GENETIC ARMAGEDDON
The Birth of Genetic Apocalypse

By

Deswin R. Gbala

Edited by Beth Groves and Kay Kutz
Cover illustration by Bob Gbala

This book is an original edition and has never been previously published.

PRINTED IN THE UNITED STATES OF AMERICA

For information contact Kay M. Kutz, Deswin R. Gbala Storytelling Comedian. 1434 George Street, La Crosse WI 54603

ISBN: 0-75961-236-6

This book is printed on acid free paper.

1stBooks - rev. 1/17/01

Sonthy Savitri

Chapter 1

The Meeting Place

My Mama and Papa lived on the northeastern border of Fridley, Minnesota, off Silver Lake Road, near by the Rice Creek Town Houses. That's where I grew up. My mother and father just flew in to La Crosse, Wisconsin from Fridley to come to my Doctorate graduation.

La Crosse is a beautiful little town with fifty thousand people. It is located on the Mississippi between two beautiful bluffs. This place is very romantic, unlike myself. I'm more pragmatic. "What can a man do for me?" I ask myself.

La Crosse and the neighboring towns of Holmen, Onalaska, and West Salem are about the biggest cities get around here. They have populations between five and six thousand. The other townships around here were unincorporated dinky towns with populations minus twenty, which all are probably relatives.

Here I am, a twenty-five year old virgin, with long legs, and very voluptuous large perky breasts. My large baby blue eyes with long eyelashes made many people envy me. They looked like paint brushes when I blink. Being the former Miss U.S.A. didn't help me any, if you know what I mean. All I get is horny pigs with little between their ears. I'm not working out and keeping my butt firm for just any idiot!

I came to the conclusion that I have to change my life. It is getting a little boring. Maybe I need some romance…nah! It is a total waste of time. I have to figure out how to replicate humans.

I used to work at the University of Wisconsin - La Crosse in Genetic Engineering. I really didn't like being a Professor. I've been sending out applications to work in the corporate world.

Mama thought it was a good idea. I've been interviewing during my off time. It's been about a year. One company, The Brotherhood Incorporated was really interested in me. I finally landed a corporate job with The Brotherhood, Inc.

Mama and I are supposed to drive to Chicago for my interview with my new boss. We decided Dad was going to take my car back to Fridley and mama and I was going to fly.

I decided that having a Computer Geek for a father really made my social life boring.

I love being with mama, she is the only exciting person in the family. She is stubborn, frisky, loud, and funny! I should have had more of my mother's personality. Maybe men are really intimidated by me, but why should they be? Jesus! How come I can understand Genetics and I don't know anything about primal functions!

Dad came and picked up the beast. It was a muscle car from the Seventies, a Chevy Malibu. It was my dad's. He thought he was going to have a boy, but I'm his only child. So he gave it to me. I wanted a Nissan, 300LX, or a Mitsubishi 3000 turbo. I was into sports cars. I like a hard stick with power to release my pent-up sexual tensions. I told mama that when we got to Chicago, the first thing I was going to do was to go shopping for a white dress and a Mitsubishi 3000 turbo! She agreed, but only on the terms that she could drive the car as often as she wanted.

I gave Papa a hug, he gave me a graduation present. Yeah, what else can you get from a computer geek for a graduation present besides a computer? Surprisingly, he gave me two computers, a Laptop and a PC. He is always giving me lectures about computers. I swear, in the past years, I think I have learned more about these funky things than Albert Einstein knows about E=MC squared. That's okay, because I love my parents. I have a big soft spot for them.

Dad took mama and me to the airport. We were going to catch American Airlines to Chicago. "Sonthy, remember to always pray and ask Jesus for help. You can never be too smart to pray. I didn't become a computer expert just from hard work honey. It was hard work and praying," dad said.

"I know, dad. I just wish you would quit lecturing me about religion, computers and everything else. You're too protective! "

Dad knew that I had a very proud and stubborn streak. He said that I would need that someday. That's why he didn't beat it out of me.

Mama was crying. Her little girl was growing up. She was so proud and protective of me. Mama was also a wee bit worried about me in the big city of Chicago, but she wouldn't say a thing. She knew better. She was coming along to check out the scene. She had to make sure that I was well provided for. I just hope this job pans out. I assured my parents that I could take care of myself. I reminded them of some of the stupid things I did. I told them about the neighbor boy who thought he was so strong. "Remember what I did to him?" Both my parents busted out laughing.

Reggie Wheat, our neighbor boy, used to come over on Saturdays, which was chore day around our house. Reggie rang the doorbell. Mama came to the door,

"Are you looking for my Sonthy?" she asked.

He blushed bright red because mama had this smirk, and did that Groucho Marx thing with her eyebrows (she moved them up and down twice), because she knew that he had this gigantic crush on me. She let him in.

"She's in the laundry room doing laundry," she said, pointing to the basement stairs.

Reggie rushed ferociously down the stairs, like a lion protecting his turf. He roared my name. He felt more connected to me. He said my name, over and over again, as he came down the stairs.

I kinda liked him I thought. He had those pudgy cheeks with dimples, and long eyelashes. Reggie thought he was the "Lion" of the neighborhood, and I was his own to conquer. I was meaning to rid him of that "*I was his*" attitude. I didn't belong to anybody, 'cept God himself. So he came down the stairs yelling my name. "Hey! Sonthy Savitri, Sonthy, Sonthy! Sonthy Savitri!"

"Yea! I'm down here doing my laundry!"

At eight years old, I was just barely tall enough to do my own laundry. I was soaking wet with blue laundry detergent all over me. It was in my hair, on my face, on the counters, on my butt.

Reggie strutted into the laundry room as if he was my king. Too much confidence, I tell ya, but that was about to leave soon.

He was an over zealous, eight year old punk, but a cute one too! Ouch! He was hot! At times I would wonder how he was doing as an adult.

My "cute punk" walked in as if he was king... When he saw me, he broke out laughing.

"Your hair, your face, but I like yo' ass!" he said, pointing at the big spot on my right butt cheek.

"Don't you be cuss'n in God's house!" I quickly reprimanded him.

"Sorry pookie, I didn't mean to cuss in God's house, Ms. Savitri." He said, and slapped my wet spot.

I loved it when he starts giving me respect, calling me Ms. Savitri. It made me proud and made me want him. I was still going to rid him of his attitude. Reggie can't just strutt into my kingdom and try to be the king. I'm the only queen and king in this laundry room, dad said I was. Dad won't even come downstairs when I'm a do'n laundry.

I never called Reggie Wheat by his real name. I always called him Cute Punk. "Hey Cute Punk," I said. "Wanna get my clothes out of the dryer?"

He stuck his head in the dryer looking for clothes. I looked down at his little legs, struggling back and forth, tipping off the ground, suddenly I had an idea. I rushed down like lighting, grabbed his legs, and pushed him into the dryer. Then, I climbed on top and pushed the "on" button. He spun around for about two minutes before I flung the door open. There he was, spinning around like a mad dog, chasing his tail in a big ball.

4

When the insides of the dryer stopped spinning, I struggled to pull him out. He was sooo clumsy! He finally plopped out on the grey carpet like The Blob.

I started laughing and said in an announcer's voice, "It's the Jell-O Blob! It is a green alien from outer space and it's going to take over the city."

Reggie started to cry. For a minute, I felt something deep inside that hurt real bad. The feeling was kinda like ripping an old patch off of your blue jeans. I just laid over him like a blanket and cried, "Mama! Papa! Can you come down stairs? I think "Cute Punk" is sick."

Dad picked him up off the floor, carried him upstairs, and laid him on the couch. Mama called his parents, and they came rushing in like a whirlwind saying, "What's wrong! What happened?"

I explained the whole story to all of them. Both sets of parents chuckled a bit, but held the laughter. I called Reggie's parent's Mr. and Mrs. Wheaties because both of them were taller than my folks. I concluded that they must have eaten a lot of Wheaties. Dad told me one time that Mr. Wheaties met his wife in college when the girl's basketball team used to scrimmage the boys. They played against each other like hungry raccoons.

I felt so bad about the whole ordeal that I visited him for a whole week, bringing him Kool-Aid, soup, candy bars, and anything that would get him to like me again. I was also grounded that whole week, too. Couldn't go outside except to visit my Cute Punk.

Reggie never did get an attitude again. He was a little afraid of me. He made me promise never to say a word to anybody. I never told a soul except for his folks and mine. His parents moved away the following year. I thought it was my fault, but Dad told me that his Papa got a new job in Waukegan, Illinois.

I thought about the past for a while, but some kid's bubble gum popped and brought my mind back to the present. So, there we were at the airport. I went to the bathroom. As I entered, I immediately went into a stall. I did my thing, and flushed the toilet. I started speaking out loud.

"I wished I had courage to go to Chicago. I'm a little scared…"

As I was talking, I heard an old woman in another stall reply to what I said. She said, "Darling, you have."

I walked out of the stalled and said, "Who are you?"

She walked out of her stall, too. She had an awful, distinct smell. The stench was like onions, mold, and alcohol. I looked at her tiny figure, her white hair, her tattered clothes, her very messy, dirty face, and finally the liquor bottle in her right hand. Her breath was saturated with that strong alcohol smell. I went to wash my hands, and watched her from the corner of my eye. She came to the other sink beside me, and started drinking water with her cupped hands from the faucet. I wondered if her hands were clean. She had just come out of the commode.

She said, in a soft, cracking whisper, "Darling you have, you must increase and I must decrease."

Then she shook her crooked tiny finger at me. I put a questioning look on my face by raising one eyebrow. For a split second, I thought about Mom and Dad waiting for me. The old drunken lady walked out the door before me. I immediately followed her. As I opened the door, I looked to my right and my left, but she was no where to be found. I thought mmm, and noted it.

I walked over to my parents. Mama was still crying, until I reminded her about Cute Punk. She and Dad broke out laughing. I reminded Dad about the time when he put me in ballet and karate for ten years, and I got my third degree black belt. I refreshed Papa's mind about Wing Chi, my competitor. I told Papa about the championship round when I beat him in the WBAK National Tournament.

I said, "Do you recall what he told me? He said, 'I fight good, you fight smart.'" I liked Wing Chi; I wonder what ever happen to him?

Dad finally gave up. He knew three things would have happened. One, I would have continued to tell him all the times I defended myself. Two, Mother would have started in on him. Three, we would have gotten in a family argument and missed the plane. So, he just quit. He really knew that I could protect myself, which was my whole point. I had to convince him that I could. Ma on the other hand didn't worry much. She knew I could take care of myself.

The 747 was ready to leave. Mom and I boarded the plane and took our seats. Soon, the plane was taxing down the runway, and then we were air- bound. The ground was falling and the airport was quickly fading.

Within five minutes of our take off, I heard the pilots say, on the overhead speakers, "we will be landing in Chicago in forty minutes. Please prepare to land. There are chocolate chip cookies outside sitting on the wings of the airplane just incase anybody's hungry from this long trip. Please feel free to help yourself. Oh, by the way, don't forget a parachute on the way out there. Have a pleasant journey, and thank you for riding with American." There was a chuckle amongst the passengers, and they continued their socializing.

I was very involved in a conversation with my mother about a project I wanted to start once I got some serious money. Mom said, "You want to call this project what?"

I said, "I want to call it 'Sister Earth.'"

Mama asked me what the project was about. We talked about 'Sister Earth,' until the plane touched down at O'Hare airport.

Mama said, "That sounds like quite an expensive adventure."

I told Mama, "It's just a dream."

Mama said, "I believe in you and all your dreams." Mama always knew how to give me warm feelings. She was my greatest support system.

Before we knew it, we were like cattle, lined up to get our luggage. I've never seen so many people in my life! They looked like millions of ants going about their business. How in the world can a girl find her way around here!? This place had moving side walks! You just stand on them and they take you to the next moving sidewalk.

Mama was just boiling with excitement. She said, "It's Chicago!, It's Chicago! Land of the Oprah Winfrey Show! I love Oprah. She has personality like Wieslesmuckle!"

I busted out laughing. Wieslesmuckle was our cat. She was a fat, white cat who purred constantly. She drew large audiences wherever we took her. Wieslesmuckle looked like a dog because she was so big, and behaved like a clown. We would put on music and she would dance and jiggle around. I never saw a cat that liked music more than I did.

O'Hare airport was our meeting place. I was supposed to meet my new boss, Alfred Zum, for my last interview. He sent me a letter, telling me I was hired, but we had to tediously go through the formalities. I was very excited and a wee bit annoyed! The job started at a quarter mill. I had thousands of reasons to be excited!

We were supposed to meet Mr. Zum at seven O'clock for dinner at Charlie's Italian Restaurant. Mom liked Italian food. Heck, Mom liked anything that was edible, as long as it didn't move around on the plate.

By the time we picked up our bags and grabbed a cab, it was about one o'clock in the afternoon, and I was starving. My stomach growled at me in anger, but I quickly barked back saying, "yea, yea, I heard ya!" We ate at McGarbage (McDonalds), then got a room at the Radisson. Our plan was to fill the hotel room full of shopping goods. This was why God made Heaven, so we can shop. I liked the simple things in life, men and shopping. With Mom, everything revolved around shopping.

We almost forgot about the seven o'clock meeting. Before we knew it, it was six! We dumped everything on the floor of our hotel room, and proceeded to freshen up. I looked in the mirror and I swear I saw a sexually frustrated animal. It almost looked human.

We rushed off to the meeting. We walked into Charlie's, and somebody was there to seat us at Mr. Zum's table. There he was sitting tall in his chair. He was about fifty-three years old, and totally bald like Telly Savalis. He had piercing blue eyes. He had on a grey, pinstriped suit. He was well composed, sipping on some kind of clear champagne.

"Hello Ms. Savitri, I am Mr. Zum," he said.

"Hi, this is my mother, Grace. I hope you don't mind that she will be having dinner with us. She leaves tomorrow afternoon at one." I said.

"Of course not," said the Zum Man. That's what everyone called him in The Brotherhood, Inc. I wonder why they called him the Zum Man. Why don't they call him Mr. Zum? He seemed like a pleasant man. I had this funny feeling that I was probably going to find out.

The Zum Man was to the point. He told me that tomorrow, after Mom left, we were going to get on a plane for Europe. Europe was where I would actually be working.

I said, "I'm ready when you're ready." We ate dinner and listened to the Zum Man tell his stories.

The Zum Man was quite amusing. We were talking about religion, and he told us one of his church experiences when he was nineteen. He said that his friend, Bill, had a muscle car. It was a nineteen sixty-nine dark blue Dodge Charger. It had a 442 under the hood. He said that they were going about ninety-five when he came squealing the tires into the parking lot of a church, called the Deliverance Temple. They called it Deliverance Temple because they cast devils out of people there. The police chased them for about three blocks and the cops squealed their cars into the parking lot of that church with five other cop cars following behind.

I just took a breath and said, "Whooo."

He continued to tell us that all of the people in the church came rushing out to see what the sirens were about. There was dark grey smoke from the tires clouding the parking lot. One of the cop cars got out of control, rear-ended another car that was following closely behind, and it was a domino effect after that. That kinda made me laugh a little.

An officer came out, yelling "Zum Man! I thought it was you! Now look what you've done!"

Zum Man told them that it was Bill's problem. It was Bill who was speeding and he would be happy to pay the fine. Then the Zum Man told the cops that running into the other cop cars was their own fault. The officers knew he was right. They gave Bill a ticket and let them go. He said that it cost Bill his "Mother's sheep," meaning it cost him a pretty penny.

The Zum Man told the police officers that he needed salvation real bad because he thought he was evil. He had to get to church immediately. That was why he told Bill to step on it, but drive professionally with supersonic caution. Since the policemen let them go, the Zum Man and Bill went into the church. When they went inside the church, the congregation sat down.

The Pastor was still trying to cast the devils out of one of the most ugliest man The Zum Man had ever seen. This man had white maggots all over his face.

When the Zum Man told us about the maggots, I quit eating my spaghetti.

He continued to tell us that the ugly man smelled like rotten pork. My nose got red and I had to pee. I told him to wait with the story until I got back. It didn't bother Ma. She just kept eating her pasta.

While I was in the bathroom, I emptied my bladder, and said, "Jesus, I know I'm praying on the pot, but please let me handle that God forsaken story."

As I said Amen, I heard a small voice that said "Amen" with me. It was a lady in the next stall.

"I just hope I don't have to fluff the sheets tonight," the woman added.

I freshened up, and returned back to the table.

"Hey, I thought the Giant Bathroom Butthead Monster swallowed you. I was about to come to your rescue," Mama said.

I said, "Nah, Ma, I'm ok. Mr. Zum can you please continue."

So Mr. Zum told us that this man was very ugly. He had nappy greasy hair that slowly crawled down to his waist. The preacher kept saying, "I cast you out in the name of the Great Deliverer."

At that, the man exploded from inside out. Pieces of human fragments sprayed over the audience. There was blood, flesh, and eyeballs hanging on the walls. The Zum Man said that maggots flew all over his face and since then he's never stepped into a church. Most of all, he wanted his head cleanly shaven. He couldn't bare the thought of maggots in his hair, that vision haunted him. Not the vision of exploding warm flesh, but maggots in his hair. So he has been bald ever since. The Zum Man began to laugh, as if he was seeing that man explode, over and over again, fresh in his mind. Unbeknownst to me, he really was.

After the Zum Man's story, I had to get some air. I excused myself, as Mama finished her food.

Mr. Zum said, "You're excused. See you at 3:00 p.m. tomorrow right here."

"Okay," I disgustingly replied.

Mom and I left very abruptly to go outside. When we were outside, I told Mom that I couldn't breathe. Actually, I could breathe fine but it felt like I couldn't. I told Mom that I liked Mr. Zum at first, but after that story, I was having doubts. Exploding men was not something that a nineteen-year-old boy should have seen. I figured that it must have had a profound psychological effect on him.

I looked up to the sky and said, "Jesus, I'm not even horny, not after that story."

Mom just laughed. She knew me well. However, she gave me a word of caution. She said, "Keep your left eye on that fella."

We both went back to the hotel around eight o'clock. Mom said, "Honey, it's only eight. Do you want to romp the town?"

I replied, "Mom, wait until Dad hears how rambunctious you've been!"

She said, I won't tell if you won't."

We both chuckled, and at the same time said, "Rock On!"

Mom rented a pearl color Mitsubitshi 3000 GL and we went into downtown Chicago to play! We looked up nightclubs in the Yellow Pages and found The Excaliber. I let Mama drive. She drove like a cheetah hunting a gazelle. She was driving so fast. If the car were black, it would have been invisible.

I was totally amazed with Chicago. It was just as busy at night as it was during the day. We had to pay seven dollars to get in. The bars in La Crosse didn't have a cover charge. You could go bar- hopping from bar to bar and it would not cost you a thing. We would stay at The Excaliber for the rest of the night.

As we walked in, I noticed that everybody was dressed up. A long hallway approached us with gold, and rounded handrails on both sides. The hallway guided us to an area with black tables, and an octagon shaped dance floor in the middle. There was an upstairs, and the center of the ceiling was open above us. There were tables and dancing holes for individuals. The music was very loud.

I told Mom, "Let's take a front table."

We sat next to the DJ both. Mom and I ordered a whole bottle of champagne, and I ordered a cheeseburger and fries. I had a hard time eating at The Zum Man's table earlier, so I was still hungry. We chattered and sipped on the champagne.

Mom told me to quit calling her "Mama," and start calling her Grace. I was supposed to be her youngest sister. Grace didn't look that old. In fact she was very pretty. She had to be, she looked like me.

"Uh, Oh," I said. "Mom, that Italian looking man has been staring at us since we got here." He was a little old for me, though. He looked to be in his forties.

He came over to our table and said to Mom in a deep, raspy voice, "You're better looking here than you were over there. So... ya wanna dance?"

A slow song was playing and Grace deviously looked at me. I nodded and shrugged my shoulders. She immediately leapt off the chair and was in his arms cheek to cheek.

I said, "Mmmm... I'm just going to finish my burger." Just as I took another bite of my burger, a handsome, clean –cut black fella asked me to dance.

I looked at him and wanted to dance, real bad, but hunger took over. I shook my head no.

"Mmm...good burger." I offered him a bite.

He politely said, "Thanks, I'm full. May I sit down?"

I said, "Sure, help yourself."

We started talking, and I noticed that he smelled real fine. It seemed like sweet cinnamon. He was so polite. He said, "See over there, that's my Pop." His voice sounded very youthful and enthusiastic. His father waved to us, I waved back. I looked at Mom on the dance floor and she was gone. She was totally beside herself.

The young man continued, "My name is Charles. What's yours?"

"I'm Sonthy," I replied.

"Do you live around here?" he said.

"No, we're just passing through," I said.

He replied, "I live in Oak Park with my parents. I just came up for the summer. I'm going to Harvard for law. Are you in school?"

"Nah, I hope not," I said.

He said, "Why don't you like school?"

I said, "Oh, I like school alright. I just finished my doctorate in genetics. I'm not about to go to school for a while."

"Wow, I'm impressed. You look so young and pretty," he said, as he softly placed his left hand on my thigh. I took a deep breath. He didn't know how much he affected my hormones when he touched my thigh. He woke up the monster.

I looked over at Mom. She was still into dancing. I think I lost her for the night. I felt my heart racing. There was a deep hunger in me that wanted to be released, like a beast in a whirlwind. I moved a little closer to Charles. I slowly leaned towards him and put my cheek near his ear and whispered, "Do you think I'm pretty?"

The edge of his lips barely touched mine. I wanted something to happen. He turned towards me a little. His soft, puffy, wet, brown lips were so delicious I could already taste them. I thought, kiss me damnit! Why don't you kiss me? His lips were softly touching mine, in a way that I didn't realize that he was already kissing me. It wasn't good enough; I wanted him to give me a deep long wet kiss. I want him to kiss me with a french kiss. Kiss me damnit! If he waited any longer, I was going to swallow him. I slowly grabbed his lower lip with my teeth, enough so he wouldn't accidentally pull away. Then, I slowly moved my hands up his thick, iron shoulders and onto his neck. I gently caressed his neck up and down, and nervously brought my hands up to his soft face. Then, I buried my tongue down his thirsty mouth. Oh yes! He reciprocated with an explosive forward thrust. I felt my thighs shake. Something between them was running like a river. I was wet with passion, a fire that made me swiftly grope his animal. Oh yes. I definitely groped his mighty glory! It was hot. I felt too much heat in this nightclub.

He said, "Do you want to go outside?"

"Yes, yes," I nodded, as if he read my mind.

We got up and started walking towards the door. I glanced at Mom. She didn't even notice that I was leaving. I stopped for a moment. I thought to myself, what am I crazy? I don't even know this man. What was I getting into?

He noticed my hesitation. He slowly put his left arm around my waist and drew me closer to him. "I wanted to, I wanted to," I kept repeating to myself.

I was trying to convince myself that I wanted to do this. I didn't even know what I was doing. I had never had sex before. I was a lost cause. I was a twenty-five- year- old virgin. Who was

14

I kidding? What if he wanted sex? I would never go through with it.

Before I knew it, I was outside, walking behind the building. Something kept my feet moving. I tried to stop them. They had their own mind. I found myself against the wall in an unceasing, passionate, engulfing kiss. Suddenly, his fingers slipped inside me. He touched a magic spot on the top of my pubic area. I thought, "What the hell was that? Do it again." Oooh, yea! He read my mind. There we were in the parking lot between the dumpster and the wall.

"Do you have a condom?" I asked.

He pulled out a Trojan Ultra-Sensitive. I opened his pants and rolled it on him, fumbling like a girl. I quickly dropped my pants. I held the garbage dumpster with my arms spread out, clamping my fingers around the edge. I felt his hands slide down my back and up my tummy, slowly caressing my breasts. Oh! I gasped for air. Oh! Oh! I was making noises that I didn't even know I could make. Oh! Hooh, uh, hooh! Uh, it was like music, a rhythm and pleasure beyond my thoughts. Oh! My God! Aha, ooooh, huh, whooo, mummmm, yea, huh. I was building; I could feel my golden kingdom! Aah, hum! Eaah, yee, ooh, yumm, harder. My God! I could see the pearly gates! Wow, oh, yea, mmm. The Hoover Dam had just busted open, and Niagara swallowed my volcano! Yes, an everlasting geyser!

We walked back into the bar, as if nothing had happened and sat down at our table. I looked over at Mama; she was dancing with that same guy. She didn't even skip a beat. Charles was sitting next to me.

He asked, "Can I get your address?"

I reminded him that I was going to London tomorrow.

I said, "Why don't you give me your address and phone number and when I get to where I'm going, I'll call you collect."

He went over to the bartender, got a piece of paper, and scribbled his full name, address, phone number, and e-mail address.

I kissed him and told him, "I have to get my mother and get to the hotel. It is three in the morning and I have a long day."

He was very sweet about the whole night. I walked onto the dance floor. I grabbed Grace's arm and brought her over to the table. I introduced her to Charles and she blurted out, "My! You're the best looking black man I've ever seen." Ma has never seen a black man, except on TV. Charles was her first encounter. She had seen them in Chicago since we had arrived, but she had never met one.

She said, "I like you. I won't tell my husband that you were talking to our daughter. He thinks black people are always getting into things." Little did ma know how correct she was in this case.

"Mama!" I yelled. "That's enough!"

She drank the entire bottle of champagne and she was a little tipsy. So, I hugged Charles and escorted Mom outside. I drove to the hotel. I helped Mama get ready for bed. I was out before my head even hit the pillow.

The next day, we returned the Mitsubishi and I saw Mom off. I always kept in contact with my parents. I loved them very much. I told Mom that I would call her, and off she went.

I checked out of the hotel and went to meet the Zum Man. It was almost three o'clock. He met me and greeted me with a nod. We walked over to American Airlines terminal and boarded our plane.

The plane took off shortly after we boarded. I found myself flying over oceans bluer than blue. I thought it was marvelous. During the whole trip, the Zum Man didn't say a word. That was good too, because I really didn't want his company. It was not like I want to be scared again. He smelt really good, even though Polo was one of my favorite colognes, I decided that I didn't like him.

Chapter 2

Europe

We landed at Heathrow Airport in London. It was an okay place. I'm not too impressed with airports, anyway. The minute I got off the plane, I looked for the fastest way out of the airport. There were a lot of people with funny sounding English accents. A black Mercedes limousine met us at the airport and took us to Westminster.

Westminister, was a very ritzy place. We headed north east on Piccadilly Street and made a right at St. James Street, then a left on Jermyn Street. Then we rode down to the Cavendish Hotel on eighty-one Jermyn Street. I got my room.

The Zum Man said I had one week to have fun in London, then it would be off to work. He gave me fifteen hundred dollars and said, "See you Sunday."

Plans automatically floated into my head. I called Mom. Ring, Ring, Ring.

Mom picked up the phone on the other end. "The Savitri's, this is Grace."

"Hi Mom!" I was excited about being in London. "Mom, did you know that... %$^**%^%$###^ &&((@!$^* ((*&&^%!!!!!!!!!!."

I rattled it off so fast Mom said, "Honey, slow down. I can't understand a word you're saying. Take a deep breath."

I sighed, "Mom, did you know that Mr. Zum gave me $1500.00 in cash to spend? He gave me a week to play. Then he said, real serious like, you know, in that deep voice of his, 'Then it's off to work.' And,... and,.. also, we drove to a hotel in Westminster in a big black Mercedes limousine. He said it was mine for a week."

Mama said, "Wow! I'm impressed. Let me get your Dad on the other phone."

"Hello, Hon," Dad said. "What's all the fuss about a big car, one week to play, and lots of cash?"

"It's true. I'm sooo, excited! Dad could you and Mom come and visit for a week? And Dad, I met a black guy. He's pretty cool."

There was some silence. Then he spoke again. "Is it serious?"

"Of course not. I met him in Chicago with Mom. Didn't she tell you?" I immediately interjected.

Dad asked mom, "Grace, why didn't you tell me she met a black man?"

This time, mom was silent. Then she said to dad, "We'll talk about it later. So you want to go see your daughter in London?"

Dad replied, "What's all the yapping Grace. What's taking you so long to pack? We will be there Sunday, Dear."

"Awesome Dad! I love you guys."

Mom replied, "You little fink!"

We both laughed. I gave them the name of the hotel and the phone number and told them to just ask for my room. Then, we said our good-byes and hung up.

It was Friday night. Mmmm, what should I do? I was hungry. I called the front desk and asked the hotel clerk to get my driver.

"I'm going out to eat. Do you have any suggestions?" I said.

The clerk said a bunch of places and I picked Mokaris Café at sixty-one Jermyn Street. I quickly jotted the number down. I called them and made a reservation.

The bathroom looked inviting before I left. My bladder was talking to me. It was saying, "Mr. Brain! Hey up there! You gonna take this body to the bathroom or am I gonna let it rip here?" I quickly shuffled into the bathroom. I washed up, grabbed my coat, and ran out.

My driver was waiting for me. When he saw me coming, he opened the rear door, and I bounced myself into the back seat. He closed the door, sat down, and off we went. He rolled down the tinted glass between the front seats and the back, then he asked me, "Where to?"

I replied, " To the Mokaris Café down the street. My reservation is not until seven; we have a half-hour. Why don't you just drive around and show me the town."

"Yes, Madam," he said. We went down St. James Street, to King Street, and ended up in St. James's Square.

The driver said, "Madam, did you notice that black Porsche that has been following us."

I quickly turned around and tried to find out what the license plate said. There wasn't one. Oh! I wonder who it is. As we drove around until seven, I periodically glanced back at the Porsche. The Porsche followed us the whole time.

My driver pulled in front of the Mokaris Café. He got out, walked around the back of the car, grabbed my door and slowly opened it. I stepped out in my red silky nightwear. My dress was styling. It was smart. It was posh. It showed every curve that wanted expression on me. I pranced to the door.

As I entered the café doors, I slowly turned around, as if in slow motion. I did this because I felt eyes burning behind my head. Somebody was staring at me. There he was. It was the man in the Porsche. The Porsche was parked on the other side of the street, parallel to the limousine. The driver window was partially rolled down. The man had on a black ski mask. We met eyes. We gazed at each other for about thirty seconds. He slowly raised a 357 magnum with a silencer to the window. He just held it there. I stood there staring back into those evil, blood-shot eyes. I was scared to death. I thought he was going to shoot me. He just sat there with that thing pointing at me.

We communicated. I silently whispered, "Oh Jesus, I'm scared to death. Whoever he is, let me look like I'm not afraid." Then I walked into the café. I hope he got my message. My feeling was, you either come out and fight like a man... or kiss my ass! What the hell kind of man hides behind the darkness? Little did I know that it was pure evil. I just wondered what he wanted. I ate my food, but it wasn't pleasant. I kept thinking about the man in that car, the Masked Man.

My driver took me back to the Cavendish Hotel. When he open my door, I looked around quickly scanning the scenery for that car. He wasn't there. I bolted to the hotel doors. I came running through the lobby and into the elevator. As I was going up, I kept thinking of those evil, blood-hungry eyes. How could anybody be so evil?

I got ready for bed. I didn't sigh until I got under my bed covers.

I whined, "Jesus, I want my Mommy." I drifted off to sleep.

I had nightmares the whole night. I remembered a clear one. I dreamt that I was a white pig being fattened for the slaughter. The farmer was Lucifer. There were two twin field workers who let demon spirits posses them. These spirits oozed out of the farmer's mouth. They entered the twins through their mouths and killed their spirits. I saw their spirits descend into a giant abyss of lava filled with flames. I saw their eyes go from nice, white eyes with beautiful blue pupils to totally black sockets with no eyes at all.

Ascending out of the abyss was another demon. This demon was a servant to the twins. The twins told this third servant demon to slaughter, at will, those pigs that were chosen. One of the possessed twins told me, the pig, to go play in the mud.

I oinked back, "No! I don't like mud." I heard myself say, "I don't care if I'm a pig, I don't like mud! I like water."

Then, the third demon grabbed me and slaughtered me. I ended up as pork chops. When I was served on plates to be eaten, I kept jumping out of people's mouths.

I abruptly woke up. It was six thirty. I was beat tired. I was dragging. I got up real quick and opened all the shades and windows. I ate a bowl of cereal in bed and just watched cartoons until one o'clock. Then, I watched romantic movies, one after another, trying to keep my mind off the dreams. I didn't go out to eat. I stayed in all day. I worked on my Sister Earth project on my laptop.

I went to bed early that night because I was tired. This time, my dreams were very sweet. I only remembered one. I remembered the one about fighting the biggest boy in the neighborhood and winning. I went up to do a back kick and I saw an angel spinning in the air with his golden wings spread out. He was doing a back kick like I was. As I came around with a spinning back kick, the angel's foot merged with mine. I kicked my opponent so hard, my foot went right through his chest cavity and squished his heart. Streams of blood came gushing out his chest, nose, and mouth.

I woke up real pumped up. I was king of my hotel room! Sunday came fast. When I awoke, I remembered that I was to pick up my parents this morning at ten o'clock. I called my driver and told him to pick me up. I was going to Heathrow Airport to get my parents.

I got dressed in white jeans and a cotton shirt. I skipped into the elevator and swished into the limousine.

"To the airport," I said to my driver. We got to the airport in perfect timing. This driver sure knew his way around.

I walked to Terminal Three. I stood there and waited for Mom and Dad to come out of the plane. Dad came out first and Mom followed. They were holding hands. That looked sweet. I wished I was married.

We got our luggage and headed outside.

Dad said, "I'm going to call for a taxi."

I said, "Dad, I have a ride. It's in front of you. Didn't you see the helpers put your luggage in the trunk?"

Mom was already in the limousine. She was motioning for him to get in. Dad just couldn't believe that his only baby could achieve this. He was a little astounded.

"Driver, take us for a tour of Westminster," I said. He just looked in the mirror and nodded.

We arrived at the hotel. There was somebody to help us bring our luggage upstairs. We finally got all settled in. Traveling can be such a headache.

We all met at the lounge bar for dinner. We decided that we were going to eat out at the Red Lion, a Victorian restaurant. It was London's few remaining gin palaces, located off Jermyn Street on 2 Duke of York Street. The menu has tasty, mouth - watering sandwiches, such as smoked salmon, tuna, and, my all favorite, the bacon, lettuce and tomato sandwich.

Mom was bubbly and vivacious. Dad was his usual, curious hum-drum self. He didn't say much. He just ate a lot.

I waited until Dad had food in his mouth and then I said, "Mom, Dad, I invited Charles to come to London. He will be arriving Monday at four. Dad, don't make his life miserable, okay? He's not coming to get lectures from you. He is coming to have fun with me." Then I cleared my throat, "Ahemmm, now, we got that clear? Do you have any comments, Dad?"

"Look Honey, you might think that I don't like black people, but that's not true. I had a Negro friend when I was in the Navy. We used to go partying. He was my best friend. He was always dating white women. I asked him why didn't he date his own kind. He just ignored me. I thought to myself that he would never date my daughter, if she were old enough. They're good to be friends with, but none of that colored stuff in my blood. It's best just left unhampered with."

I rolled my eyes and sort of tuned out. I was somewhere between Jupiter and Saturn. I wasn't quite at Pluto, but if he kept talking, I would be. That was just Dad, though. I mean, I loved my dad, and all, but mom was more fun. She was daring, creative, risky, she's just a down right trouble maker! In a good way I mean. She didn't get into trouble with the law, or nothing like that. She just drew a lot of attention to herself. One time, she made me laugh so hard, I was bawling. Every time she would walk in the room, my stomach was ready to laugh. Let me just call her, "high spirited!"

Mom said, "Honey, don't pay no mind to what your Dad's saying. He's just being frumpy."

After dinner, we decided to go see *Star Wars: The Phantom Menace* at the Jermyn Street Theatre on 166 Jermyn Street. The limousine pulled up to the theatre. Everybody was looking at us. They thought I was some big star or something. I thought it was more the "something."

As we were pulling up, I noticed that black Porsche. The Man in the Mask had been following me again. I noticed that the driver didn't say anything about him this time. I was glad, too. I didn't want to have my folks fussed up. There was not any sense worrying about stupid things. If one was going to worry, either worry about it after you are dead, or don't worry about anything at all, except if you got your makeup on right. That's important.

My girl friend, Tracy, used to say, "When I look at myself in the mirror in the morning, I have a hard time looking at that face without makeup. A woman has to put on a little eye shadow and some blush. I don't want to burden other people's eyes looking at uncultivated beauty. Sometimes in the morning, I think when God looks at me, he puts on his sunglasses."

Sometimes, it's hard for me to relate to Tracy. I think makeup is good every now and then, especially when you're going out, but to worry about it just to get you out the door every morning is "dogging!" So, if that man wanted to kill me, let him. He had been following the car a couple of times now. He should have already killed me, if he is any professional at all. There is no way I was going to have another sleepless night. He could just go fuck himself!

Watching the *Phantom Menace* was interesting. It had so many special effects. My eyes did not have enough time to enjoy all those animations. Dad was really into it. It was the only time you would ever see Dad excited. He got all worked up when it came to *Star Wars*, and *Star Trek*. He got excited about anything with science in it. He was a sci-fi freak! Sometimes, if he knew ahead of time that we are going to see a particular sci-fi movie, he would wear a costume from one of the characters in the movie. It was so embarrassing. This kind of attention sat with me like rotten eggs, kind of like a turd in a punch bowl. If mom was to do something like that, she would be subtle about her costume. She may just wear a tiny piece of jewelry from a movie or an eloquent dress. She would never wear a freaking monster suit, like Dad did when we went to see *Godzilla.*

Mom thought *The Phantom Menace* didn't have a strong plot. I didn't think it did either. It didn't even build the characters like it did in the first movies. I actually got attached to Harrison Ford as Han Solo. *The Phantom Menace* had lots of glory but no guts. Dad tells me that back in the States people still wait overnight to see the *Phantom Menace.* Oh boy!

We got back to the hotel and we called it a night. Mom and Dad went to their suite and I to mine. As soon as I walked in, the phone started ringing. I picked it up and said, "Hello, this is Sonthy."

"Sonthy, this is Charles," the voice said. Charles continued, "I'm calling you from the airplane. I'm just letting you know I'll be on schedule."

I told him, "That's good. I'll be there to pick you up Monday at four, bye-bye." I hung up the phone.

Charles was a good communicator. He was very sensitive, and thoughtful.

The morning came fast, and I kept on sleeping. I slept like a rock. What woke me up was a knock on my door. I was a little sluggish, but very rested. "Honey, are you in there?" It was Mom.

"Hold on a minute, Mom, I'm coming!" I put on my robe and dazed over to the door. I rubbed my eyes with my left hand as I opened the door with my right. "Come in, mom. What's the matter?"

Mom replied, "Nothing. It's ten o'clock; you're sleeping so late. I thought I'd check on you. Your father and I already had breakfast. I'll call up some breakfast for you while you get ready."

"Thanks Mom." Mom always knew when to do things. She always had good timing for everything. I got out of the shower and dressed, quickly. Mom put my hair in a ponytail. I thought that was good. It would keep me cool. I sat down to eat my blueberry pancakes that Mom had ordered. She sat across the table from me. "What's Dad doing?" I asked.

Mom replied, "He's working on his laptop on your Sister Earth project. He's really excited about it. Since you told him five years ago about that crazy idea, he's been working on it during his spare time. How's your end going?"

"Really great, mom. I get excited too. I'm so glad dad gave me this state- of- the- art laptop. The animation software really helps me with my planning."

"That's good, Dear. I'm proud of you. You just keep up the good work. Norbert is proud of you, too."

"Mom, why did dad give me his name? I don't want to be called Sonthy Norbert Savitri."

Mom responded, "He thought if you had a boy, that he could take your middle name, which, in turn, will take your dad's name. And we will have us a Norbert, Jr. He named you that when the doctor told me I couldn't have any more children."

I replied, "The cheese stands alone on this one, for now. I don't even have a boyfriend."

Mom replied, "Charles is coming."

I said, "I know Mom, but it's too early, yet." I quickly changed the subject. "So, have you thought of what you want to do today? You know this evening I'm planing to spend with Charles. I figure, when he comes, you and Dad can have the evenings alone together. But I'll hang with you guys all day. Charles can keep himself busy until evening. I told him that you guys were here."

Mom was eager to reply. She said, "That's very, very good, Honey. Maybe I can give your Dad some CPR in the theatre!"

We both laughed. "Speaking of Dad, I'll give him a call," I said. I dialed the phone.

Dad's phone rang. He picked it up and said, in his nasal phone voice, "Hello."

I replied, "Dad, can you come over?"

"Sure thing, Honey. Be right there." We hung up.

Dad was a very punctual person. The minute he hung up the phone he was zooming down the hall and knocking on my door. Mom let him in. Dad hustled in and said, "Let's rock the town; I'm feeling a bit frisky!"

Mom and I both raised an eyebrow. We hurried out the door and crunched into the elevator. As we were getting out of the elevator in the lobby, I said, "Remember, I will go get Charles in the limousine by myself, then I'll meet you here at five and we can go out to eat. And Dad, no fussing with Charles! Mom, tell him that's an order." Mom just gave Dad that look: that wrinkled eyebrow look that said, "You better behave."

The driver arrived. He opened the back door of the limousine as we approached it. We piled in like bowling balls, one after another. The driver drove to Westminster Harbor.

We walked around looking for a sailboat to rent. We were going sailing on the wild seas! We rented a sailboat called Lady Quail. The captain's name was Mr. Ice.

Dad was rambunctious. He was into this sailing stuff. We sailed on the North Sea. It was rough, but wild. Mother was excited to see dad in a different spirit. He wasn't even himself. He was running around the deck, holding onto the rails, and yelling, "Away she goes!" His eyes turn bluer than I have ever seen them. Excitement went through him like bolts of electricity. Mom watched him like the first time they met, all in love with glossy eyes. I was glad to see mom and dad happy. Maybe we could go sailing again, Friday.

We docked the boat. I called the limousine from the boat to let him know that I wanted to go to the airport to pick up Charles. The driver was very polite. We dropped mom and dad off at the Hotel. Mom and dad were smooching in the back the whole time we drove to the hotel. I was a little embarrassed. It was nothing I could not handle. They used to smooch like that ten years ago. I just hoped dad would not lose his zeal. His zeal was always linked to his phenomenal performances. That's what mom told me. I could never picture them doing it. That's an ackeepoody-icky thought. I'm glad I took the job. It was bringing my folks closer.

The limousine arrived at the airport. Charles was already waiting for me. He said, "The plane landed early."

I walked over to him with excitement. I knew I would be getting some. He leaned over to kiss me and I bent over and grabbed some of his luggage. He missed the kiss. Not that I didn't want to kiss him; I wanted to real bad, but my body was for me to do as I would, not to be kissed or groped at another's beckoning. I had to make my point clear to him. If we were going to do any playing, it was going to be on my terms. If he didn't like it, he knew where the airport was.

He knew just what to say. He said, "Can I help you with your luggage?"

I started to laugh. I looked up at him as I stood up. He was grinning. He had that sexy grin. I replied with a growl. That put him at ease. Things were a little tense. I wasn't expecting my reaction. But it was nice to see him again. He, on the other hand, was excited and comfortable.

We slipped into the limousine. He sat next to me. He sat so close there wasn't enough air to breath, not even for an air molecule to pass through. I got up and went to the seat behind the driver. I said, "Look Charles, when I had sex with you in Chicago, it was my first time. I was a virgin. You're the first man I have ever been involved with. I've never even kissed a man before. So just don't get too friendly."

He looked at me in surprise. His cute eyebrows were up. His eyes were wide open like big brown cow eyes. His mouth just hung open, totally speechless. He didn't say a word for about ten minutes. Boy, do I have a way with men. I felt so stupid after I said that. He was just stunned. I felt a little awkward.

I prayed inside, "Ok, Jesus you got to help me here. What the hell did I get myself into?" Then I leaned over and caressed his hand a little.

I said, "Charles, my body is for me to do as I will, not for you to grope at your pleasure. I set the rules here. If you don't like it, you know where the airport is. I'm not experienced with men, nor am I good with them. You need to back off a little. Do you understand where I'm coming from?"

He sighed. "Wooo, that was intense," he said.

"But I feel better," I said.

He continued with relief, "Hope we can have some fun sight seeing and rocking the joints." I smiled and giggled like a little girl. He chuckled and said, "You know what?"

"What?" I replied.

"That was my first time, too. I would go on these dates and have all the foreplay, but never could go through with actual penetration. I was too scared. I didn't even know what happened in Chicago. But after we were done, I started to cry. I cleaned up when you were getting your pants on. I was too ashamed to tell you that it was my first time. I feel so relieved to hear you tell me that it was your first time, too. I hope we can be friends."

I said, "Oh, yeah, we'll be friends all right. I still want to get that hard thing out of your pants and into mine. I'm just feeling a little awkward right now."

He looked at me in surprise. He said, "Do you really?"

"Oh, yeah!" I said. I rolled the dark window up between the driver and us. I came over to him and got his animal out and started kissing it. I licked it softly. I was engaged with desire. I undid myself and sat right on it. It hurt at first. I started moving up and down. I felt it now. Ooh. The long, thick, smooth member was really hard and it went deep. Mmm, huh, huh, huh, oh, huh, harder, mmm, harder, yea, ho, hea, oh God. Mmm, oh, oh, oh, oh, yea, huh, oh, yea, mm, do it! Huh. My Hoover Dam exploded! What's going on? I hopped on again. Oh, huh, yea, oh baby, yum, mmm, yum, oh yea, mmm. Faster, there you go, huh, mmm, yea, grunt. I felt the gush. The space shuttle has exploded into space! Yea!

The limousine reached the hotel. We took his luggage up to his suite. His was next door to mine. We had a door that went between our suites. I planned this. I wanted easy access into his room in the middle of the night when I rolled over onto my stomach, and felt the urge, and that little magic spot was encouraged. When it gets happy, I would have to bust into his room. I thought I planned it pretty well.

I called my parents' room to let them know that we had arrived. They were playing chess. Dad had just beat mom, again. Dad would always beat mom, but mom kept on playing. I think she was just entertaining him.

Mom answered the phone, "Hello, it's Grace."

"Mom, it's me."

"Oh, hello Dear!" she said.

"Mom, Charles is here. Would you like to meet him?" I said.

"Sure, Honey. Dad and I will meet you downstairs in the lobby," she politely said.

"Okay, bye." I hung up the phone.

Dad had the chess board set up again. He was ready to play another game. They would play sets of twenty-five games. Mom would get beat so fast that Dad would be ready to beat her again.

Mom told Dad, "Charles is here." Dad just grunted. Mom told him he needed to get up and come downstairs because he was going to meet Charles. He grunted again, but went along.

Charles and I were sitting in the lobby across from each other, talking about science when Dad and mom came in. Mom greeted Charles in her usual, charming way. She placed both hands over his, and said, "Pleased to meet you again, Charles."

Charles said, "Thank you. It's good to see you again. I see why Sonthy is so beautiful."

Dad shook his head in disgust. Then it was his turn to greet Charles. He shook his hand very abruptly and said, "I'm hungry, let's eat something."

I looked at Charles. He nodded yes.

Dad wanted to go to the Red Lion, we got into the limousine. Dad and mom sat together behind the driver, and Charles and I sat next to each other.

The phone rang. I said, "Dad would you pass me the phone." He answered, "Yea."

I listened. It was the driver. I listened some more. Then I hung up. The driver wanted me to know that the black Porsche was on the left. I wound the window down a little. I peeked out.

Mom asked, "Is anything wrong dear."

"No, mama. I told the driver that I liked sports cars when we first met," (which I actually did tell him) "so he just called to let me know there was one beside us and for me to check it out."

"Oh, that was nice of him," she said.

Dad and Charles didn't sense anything wrong, but I know Mama did. It was her "mother's intuition" again. She wouldn't have said that if her "mother's intuition" weren't kicking in. She was right, but I made light of it. I just ignored the Porsche when we arrived at the Red Lion. The black Porsche was parked across from us on the other side of the street. The driver was in there with the window partially rolled down. His gun was pointed at me again, but I knew he wasn't going to shoot. Maybe he was just waiting for the right timing. Why would he want to kill me anyway? I haven't been in Europe very long, and I'm not anybody important. Maybe the limousine gave him the impression that I was somebody important. Even if I was important enough, wouldn't he want to kidnap me, instead of pointing that silly thing at me? Like I had said before, I was just going to ignore him.

We took our seat in the Red Lion. Dad was actually polite to everybody. I was amazed. We ordered our food. The food took a little time, but it was just in time to save Charles from my dad's steel claws. Dad kept scanning Charles. It was like two dogs sniffing each other's behinds. Charles was checking out dad, too. He had met mom in Chicago. He liked mom. He thought she was pretty and high-spirited. On the other hand, Charles didn't know Dad very well, and didn't want to know him. Dad didn't lecture him, but made him uncomfortable.

Finally, Mom said, "Norbert, quit that." Mom usually calls him dad, but when she called him Norbert, one knew it was serious.

Charles whispered to me. He said, "Looks like your dad is being chastised for a no-no."

"Yea, he deserves it, too!" I said.

We started eating. The food was outstanding. There wasn't much talk when we were eating. After we finished eating, dad became more human. He must have been as hungry as a Tyrannosaurus Rex. I could just imagine dad, as a Tyrannosaurus, tearing his teeth through the flesh of goats and cows from *Jurassic Park*. That made dad the most ugliest Tyrannosaurus that had ever lived!

I looked at dad as he was eating his food and said, "Dad you remind me of that mean Tyrannosaurus in *Jurassic Park*." He looked up, grunted, and went back to eating.

When Charles heard me say *Jurassic Park*, he just forgot about dad and started jabbering about the movie. He said, "Next to *Star Wars,* that's got to have the best animation I've ever seen! I love sci-fi movies. *Star Wars* is my all time favorite. Darth Vader is my favorite character. The first time I saw that movie, I bought a Darth Vader costume and wore it to the movie!"

Charles was very excited now. I put my hand on his shoulder and said, "I think you're too excited. You're going to fly off your chair." He kept unknowingly standing and sitting, standing and sitting when he got excited.

He continued, "My dad bought me this laptop that I take to the movies with me. I keep all the information about the characters on it. Then, I can look things up and comment on the movie as I'm watching it. This way I don't forget my thoughts. Dad was into building computers. He has his own business building computers, and selling software. I can remember tearing my first computer apart when I was four. I build my own now. But Sci-fi movies are my favorite."

He was talking so much and so fast, his topics were jumping from place to place. It was a little hard to follow him. Now dad, on the other hand, followed him well.

Dad said, "Do you wear costumes to movies too? So do I! I do software for a living. I'm a computer programmer."

"No shit," Charles said.

Dad said, "No shit!"

Mom cleared her throat to remind them that they were in the presence of ladies. You wouldn't believe what movie we saw after dinner. Yup! *Star Wars: The Phantom Menace.* Dad and Charles wore costumes. Charles brought his laptop, and mom and I slept. We brought our little pillows.

The movie was over. Afterwards, Charles and dad talked until three o'clock in the morning. Mom came to my suite and slept there. We lost the boys for the night. That kind of ruined my night rendezvous plan, but I slept like a baby. Mom was up, and breakfast was already on the table. There were fringe benefits to having Mom stay overnight. Mom and I talked and hung out in my suite until the boys got up. I thought dad was going to eat Charles for breakfast. Dad had me worried a little. I thought he was going to make the next three to four days miserable. It was Tuesday.

The phone rang. It was dad. He wanted to know if mom was coming home. Mom hugged me, and I kissed mom. She closed the door behind her when she went over to his suite. Then, the phone rang. I picked it up.

"Hello," I said.

"I want you to be ready Monday morning at five o'clock. The car will take you to the Helo Pad." It was the Zum Man.

"Ok," I said. His voice gave me the creeps. I hung up.

Then, the phone rang again. It was mom.

"Hi, Dear. Just call us when you're ready to go sight seeing. What have you arranged with Charles?" she said.

I replied, grumpily, "He didn't call yet."

"Have you thought about calling him, Dear?"

"Yea," I replied.

"Well why don't you?"

I said, "He'll call me, mom. I don't want to seem too anxious to talk to him."

Mom raised her voice a little, as she does when she gets excited, and said, "Ah, hog wash! You're young! Quit wasting time! You want to get old before you have fun? I know you're going to get some from that boy!"

I replied, "Mom, remember that night in Chicago…."

"You didn't," She said.

"Did too. And I did again in the limousine coming back from the airport … twice. Mom, it's like a drug! " I said.

"I know dear. Your dad wanted some. That's why he called me over."

"That rascal!" I said. I continued, "Ok, mom, I'll call him. Bye."

She hung up. The phone rang as soon as I hung it up.

I picked it up, and said, "The county Zoo!" That's what I felt like. I had been on the phone since dad called.

It was the front desk. "Ma'am, your driver came and said he is going to eat. He'll be back in an hour," said the lady.

"Thanks for telling me." I hung up the phone. It rang again. "Hello, it's the Late Show with Sonthy Sa…vi……try!" I figured if the phone was going to keep ringing, I might as well entertain myself.

It was Charles. "Hi, I like your greeting."

"Hi, Charles. Hey, you want to meet at about four?" I asked.

He said, "That will be fine."

"See you at four then. Bye."

I hung up the phone. Then, it rang again. I walked out of the room. I was sick of the phone. I walked to mom and dad's suite. I knocked hard.

Mom opened the door. "There you are dear." She said. She continued, "Your dad was just calling you." Then, she yelled to dad, "Sonthy is here, dad!" Dad came happily around the corner. I knew he had got some. It must have been good. He had a big smile.

We decided to go boating again. It was wild. I love the North Sea. We saw Cetaceans, lots of them. That's what Mr. Ice called Killer Whales.

I met Charles at four. I told him my dad liked him.

Charles quickly replied, "I like your dad, too. He reminded me of my own father. Your dad has a peculiar sense of humor."

I knew that, I thought, it's good that other people can discover my father.

We got in the limousine. I said to the driver, "Take us to the best dance club in London."

The driver said that the Bar Rumba nightclub is open from ten o'clock at night to to three o'clock in the morning. We had to eat dinner anyway, so we went to European Dine. Ah, the food was great! They made a fuss over us. We ate like pigs. Charles tried to talk romantic to me. I told him to cut the idle talk. I thought it was bullshit. Here I am, trying to eat a good supper, soft music playing, the lights are dimmed, and there are candles on the table! I was trying to savor life.

All of a sudden his voice got real soft like. He started saying, "Every time I look at you, all I think of is your beauty. It flows like the evening sunset. When I hear your voice, I hear a symphony of poetry. I see my children in your eyes dancing around your rainbow of love…"

First, I laughed. I let him make a fool of himself for a while, then I finally told him to shut up. I told him to talk normal or don't talk at all.

He said, "What's wrong?"

I said, "I don't believe in words of enchantment. They're only for those who have a strong hunger to be loved. I have no such need. I'm motivated by objectives. I set my goals, and I do it. Women that desperately need to be loved believe such fluffy words."

He argued his point. He said, "I was feeling romantic!"

I said, "Speaking junk is your idea of romantic? My idea of romance is sitting on a rock that is on top of a cliff by the ocean. Then, watching the sun set. Romance is an appreciation for life and beauty. It's a disposition that comes from a heart that is true. You can't talk junk to me. I can tell that your heart is not in it."

Charles looked at me with perplexity. He said, "Am I transparent or something? How can you see through me?"

I said, "Let's just put it this way, Mr. Harvard Man, I listen with my heart. I pay attention."

Charles said, "Is that kind of like women's intuition?"

I said, "Never mind. It's just something you cultivate within yourself. Are you ready to dance and sweat?"

"I'm up for that!" he said enthusiastically.

We finally arrived at Bar Rumba. We had to pay twelve pounds to get in. The music was loud. We went upstairs. I've never seen a bar so large. There was wall to wall people, like sardines in little outfits. It was smokey, too. Between the smoke from the cigarettes and the smoke that came from the dry ice, this place was like driving in New York! I was going to have to get used to this. Charles felt right at home. He was thinking that some of the girls looked very pretty. He should have known that he had the best looking one in the place by his side. He was checking out some woman with extremely large breasts. There was a bunch of men surrounding her on the dance floor. She was just shaking it. I wanted to dance, but Charles kept looking at that lady. He didn't notice me walk away onto the dance floor. This big fellow asked me to dance, so I accepted. He and I were bumping and grinding. We were getting nasty! Ouch! He was hot!

That lady with the super breasts noticed Charles watching her. She walked off the dance floor and came to him. He was smooth. He just feasted his eyes on her cleavage. They started to talk. They talked for about two hours. He still had not noticed I was now sitting at a table with Husky. Husky was very blonde and was an awesome dancer. When he danced, I could see the passion in his thighs.

He started to try to seduce me. I told him, "No thanks. I'm just having fun."

The big-busted woman asked Charles to go home with her; she wanted some noogie. Charles told her that he had a date. But when he looked around to see me... I was not by his side. Like I was going to stand by his side until he was ready to have fun. That was mud! He excused himself politely from the woman and started looking for me.

When he found me, he saw that Husky had his hands all over me. I pushed him away. I said, "Look Husky, I'm just here to have fun." That was when Charles arrived. He was boiling with fuming jealousy. He pushed the man. Then, Husky decked him a good right in his jaw. Charles fell. Well, that just pissed me off!

I screamed "Hey! That's my man! What the hell do you think you're doing! I'm going to have to whip your ass."

Husky laughed. He said, "You whip my ass?" Charles was still on the ground. He was out cold. I don't think he was much of a fighter. By now there was a large crowd around us. The bouncers came, but stopped. I told the bouncers not to interfere, because his blonde ass was about to get destroyed. By this time the music was off. The whole bar was silent. Husky took a swing at me. I did the splits, and his punch missed me. But my punch landed on his jewels. I stood up quickly while he stumbled around and held on to his crotch grunting. He got angry and rushed me. I moved to the side and elbowed him in the back. He fell on some ladies. The bouncers picked him up and threw him back in the circle. As he was just turning around, his face met my spinning back kick. He fell on his back, and I jumped on him and punched his face with wild flurries.

He finally passed out. I stood up. Everybody started clapping for me. I just ignored them. I splashed a glass of cold water on Charles face. That woke him up real fast. I took him outside. The driver helped me put him in the limousine.

We went home. I kissed his boo-boo and told him he was going to be all right. I explained the whole thing to him on our way to the hotel. He thanked me. When we got to the hotel, I noticed that black Porsche again. The window was cracked open and his gun was pointed at me. I turned around and gave him the finger.

Charles was still feeling a little light headed. I helped him to his room. He got undressed and went to bed. I went to my suite. I hung a sign on the door that said "Do Not Disturb."

It was a rough night. I fell into a deep sleep that night. I woke up about five o'clock to empty my bladder. When I was finished, I went to lie down, but I couldn't get to sleep. I was already well-rested for some odd reason. I turned on my stomach and that little magic spot on my pubic area started to come to life. OOOh, that felt sooo good. I pushed my pelvis deeper into the mattress. Mmmmm. I kind of went in circles with my hips. Then I couldn't help it. I slowly reached into my panties and touched my magic spot. I rubbed it in circles. My eyelids slightly closed. I could feel my deep breaths shoot pleasure through me. That's it. Ah, it felt so good.

I could not stand it. I got up off my bed and opened the inner door to Charles suite. Charles heard me come in and woke up. He got up and greeted me. He asked me if anything was wrong. I just planted him a deep, wet kiss on his lips. I ran my hands over his chest. I explored his abdomen with my tongue. I licked my way to his hard, smooth, golden treasure. His treasure was throbbing as I swallowed it into my mouth. He was moaning. His fingers were slowly rubbing my smooth bottom. He slowly slipped his fingers into my moist well, then slowly started to penetrate in and out. I kissed him wildly, like a frantic puppy. We flopped on his bed. We rolled back and forth, up and down, licking, sucking, tasting, eating, and caressing. I laid on top of him. I slowly reached down and placed his hot rock inside of me. My breast cleaved to his chest. I kissed him madly, passionately, as I thrust my pelvis forward and backward. Deep into me he went. The tip of his golden treasure touched something at the bottom of my well. I started to shake and quiver. My thighs went limp as they continued to shake. I moaned, mmmm, aah, yes, yes, do it. Don't quit. He was on top now, in the traditional position. Back and forth he thrust. Deeper, my mouth was open, my back was arched, and my chin was back. I squeezed his back and clawed it. Ooh, huh, more, yes, huh, huh, mmm, harder. I let out a high-pitched pleasure scream. My whole body started to quiver and shake. It rushed up through me. I saw the explosion of the sun. My muscles went limp. That morning we slept, for the first time, in each other's arms.

I heard my phone ring in my suite. It was ten o'clock. I quickly got up, put on my panties and ran to my suite. I picked up the phone. It was mom. She said, "Hello Dear, did I wake you?"

I said, "Huh?" I was still sleepy. "Hi, mom."

Mom was excited for some reason. She said, "Your father is in an extremely good mood this Saturday morning. He wants to know if we can go sailing again. He said he has been anticipating sailing since we last went. There was something on the news about killer whales around the area where we were sailing. Your dad wants to go see them. He says to bring Charles. He likes him."

I said, "Did I hear that right. Dad wants me to bring Charles?"

Mom replied, "That's right, Dear. Bring Charles."

I answered, "Well, I'll call him to see if he's interested."

In her usual, loving voice mom said, "I'll be over in ten minutes to bring you your breakfast. Your dad and I just came back from eating. I brought you something to eat."

That's my mommy! I'm so proud of her. I'm proud to be her daughter. Nobody could have such a beautiful, loving mom. I always got teary eyes when I thought about mom. I finally replied, "Okay! See you in a little bit. Bye." We hung up the phone.

I quickly dialed Charles number. It rang.

"Charles here," he answered.

"Hi Charles. It's me, Sonthy. Dad wants you to go sailing with us. Are you game?"

He replied, "I'm in; be over in an half hour."

I was just eating when Charles arrived. He was about to give me a hug. I pushed him away and took another bite. Mom looked at me with a big grin. She knew we had been doing the wild thing last night. She could tell. I motioned Charles to sit down.

Mom picked up the phone and called dad. Dad picked the phone after one ring. "Norbert." He said.

"Honey, it's me. Charles is here. Are you coming? Sonthy is almost finished eating."

Dad replied, "Be there, I'm almost finished with what I'm doing. I'm working on the Sister Earth project. Okay, I'm closing my file on the laptop. See you in a minute. Bye."

Dad was over before I even finished brushing my teeth. Dad was happy to see Charles. He greeted me with a kiss on the cheek. He took one look at Charles and said, "Hey there son! What happened to your face? Were you chasing my daughter and she smoked you?"

Charles answered, "Not exactly." I told dad I would explain it on the way down. Mom kept on grinning as we all left my suite. She slapped me on my tush as I closed the door behind me. That was mom's love pat. It meant good work. She was talking about the sex that I had last night. Dad, of course, didn't have a clue.

We took the limousine to Westminster Harbor again. We called ahead from the limousine to let Mr. Ice know we wanted to take Lady Quail out. When we arrived, Mr. Ice had Lady Quail ready. We just got on board and away we went. Dad was in his own world now. He and Charles were conversing the whole way down to the boat. Dad walked to the front of the boat and sat down. The air was cool and breezy. Mom, Charles and I hung out in the bow and just talked about the beautiful sea.

Mr. Ice said, "I'm taking you to where those killer whales are. You know the place that was on the news. Every reporter with television cameras will be there! It's supposed to be a rare occasion."

I yelled up to dad and told him what Mr. Ice had said. Dad just motioned his index finger to his lips. He wanted me to be quiet. He already knew about the event of the killer whale migration. He saw it on the news this morning.

We arrived at the place. There were huge killer whales coming up for air all over the place. The British Coast Guard was there. There were reporter boats, police boats, and spectator boats everywhere. Dad fetched his video camera and started shooting. He was so excited that he stood up.

He was leaning against the rails to get some good shots. Then a wave came and tipped the boat. Dad fell over the railing and into the water. He cut his leg on the railing. There was bright red blood in the water. One of the Cetaceans (killer whales) was swimming over to him. I think it smelled the blood trail in the water.

Mom was yelling hysterically. She said, "Norbert, hold on Norbert! Mr. Ice is calling for help."

Dad was pawing through the water just to keep afloat. Dad didn't know how to swim very well. Charles dove into the water to help him. Dad was crying. I felt so bad. There was nothing I could do, except hang onto to mom. She wanted to jump in, too. The Coast Guard came over to help him out of the water.

Before we knew it, the reporter boats were there, also. Cameras were all over the place. They were pulling dad out when a killer whale came up for air and took a large bite out of my dad's bleeding leg. One of the other boats pulled up Charles. It was harder to pull dad up because he was crying and yelling, but they got him up just in time before that killer whale came around for seconds.

My heart about jumped out of my chest when I saw dad's leg. It was tore completely off. The flesh was dangling, the blood was spraying all over the water, and I could see the white cartilage and bone. It was an awful sight. Mom started crying. Reporters were filming and taking pictures. There was a huge commotion. It ruined our day. Dad and mom were supposed to catch their flight that day at ten o'clock in the evening. The boats took dad to the hospital.

When we got to the hospital, the reporters were there. The place was a zoo. Dad was in emergency surgery. I told them we were his family. They let us through. We had to wait in the surgery waiting room until dad was done. Mom was pacing. A nurse gave Charles some hospital gowns so he could get out of his wet clothes.

They told us dad was missing everything from the knee down. I knew that, but mom didn't know. She turned her head when dad came out of the water. She would freak out whenever she would see blood. Mom was just pacing back and forth with a kleenex in her hand. She was still crying. I just let her pace. I held Charles hand. We just sat there and waited. Charles didn't say a word.

After two hours, they brought dad into the recovery room. The doctor came over and said he was going to be fine. If he would have stayed in that water ten minutes more, he would have died. But the good news was that he was well. He would be up in a half-hour.

They took us to a room. About fifteen minutes later they brought him into a room. Mom sat and held his hand until he woke up. His vital signs were strong. The doctor talked with us to reassure us things would be fine. He would get some crutches to go with him. We waited another couple of hours until they knew he was ready to leave. A nurse's aid helped us get him into a wheelchair and helped us get him into the limousine. Dad was very quite. He didn't say a thing all the way to the suite.

We were all in mom and dad's suite, when the phone rang. Mom picked up the phone. She said, "H-H-Hello."

It was the front desk. They said, "Hello. Is this Mrs. Grace Savitri?"

Mom replied, "Yes it is."

"Madam, the press is down here because Queen Elizabeth II is in the lobby, asking to see Norbert Savitri."

Mom said with hesitation, "I... I will be right down. Bye." She hung up the phone. "Sonthy?" Mom said with a little confusion. "Will you come downstairs with me? The hotel said Queen Elizabeth II is downstairs. She wants to see dad."

I was surprised. I replied, "Huh, can you repeat that?"

Again Mom said, "Queen Elizabeth II is downstairs in the lobby. She wants to see our Norbert. Will you come with me, please?"

Still surprised, I replied, "Of course, mom." I looked at Charles who was sitting on the sofa listening. His mouth was wide open. One of his eyebrows was up. He was in complete astonishment and confusion.

I said to Charles, "Could you tell dad that we went downstairs because the Queen wants to see him? And can you just keep an eye on him until we get back? Please help him with what ever he needs."

"Sure thing," said Charles.

Mom and I went downstairs. Immediately upon arriving in the lobby, the Queen's security guards came to escort us. They escorted us to the Queen. She was sitting in a special chair brought in by her staff. It was solid gold. She had diamonds all around her neck. She even sat like a Queen. The press was taking pictures all over the place.

We shook her hand and said, "Hello, your Majesty."

She was very kind. The Queen replied, "Is King Savitri doing well?"

Mom and I looked at each other at the same time. The same thoughts were going through our heads. I thought, King Savitri?

Mom cautiously replied, "My Norbert is fine. He is upstairs watching the news." Of course, dad was watching the live broadcasting. He was watching us talk to the Queen of England!

The Queen said, "May I have a word with him? I heard from the royal press that his leg was eaten by a Cetacean."

Mom said, "Can I make a call?"

One of the security men handed mom a cellular phone from his pocket. Mom called dad. The phone rang. Charles picked it up. "Hello, this is Charles,"

Mom said, "Charles, this is Grace, can you put my husband on the phone please?"

Charles replied, "Yes Ma'am." Charles walked over to dad, who was sitting across from him on the sofa, and handed him the phone.

Dad answered, "Hello."

Mom said, "Honey, Dear, it's Grace. Is it ok to bring the Queen up?"

Suddenly, dad forgot about his leg. He thought it was still there. He couldn't believe that it was gone. Dad said, "Well Grace, Haley's Comet will pass by the time you bring her up. What's taking so long? I've been watching you on the news."

Mom hung up the phone and nodded okay. Security took us upstairs first. They didn't want us in the same elevator as the Queen. Then she came up with a mob of people. The whole hallway was covered with people. Security kept the press outside in the hallway.

We escorted Queen Elizabeth to the sitting room. Dad was sitting on the sofa. A security person motioned for him to remain seated. They cleared an area and put the Queen's chair down. Then she gracefully sat down.

She said, "Salutations, King Norbert Savitri the IV. How are you feeling with that leg?"

Dad did a double take. He looked at his leg, looked at the Queen, looked at his leg again, then looked at Mom, and finally me. We shrugged our shoulders. After a long pause, he said, "Who's King Savitri?"

She handed him a couple of documents. One was his birth certificate from the Island of Patmos. The second one was a letter from Grandpa in Patmos. I thought all those stories that he told me about Grandpa being a King were just fairy tales. Dad thought they were, too. An American family adopted him when he immigrated to America. He said his adopted father told him these stories when he was young. He never believed them. He didn't believe them even when he grew up. Except there was one problem. There was a Queen sitting in his suite calling him King.

Dad looked over all the papers, then looked up at the Queen. Dad said, "Is this true?"

The Queen replied, "Your Majesty, I'm afraid so. Your real father passed away about three years ago. We have been trying to locate you since his death. Now, you are King of the Island of Patmos."

Dad said, "If that's true, can you call President Bill Clinton on your royal phone and let me talk to him? I want to go home. I want to go to my American home."

The Queen nodded to her security and they made the arrangements. It took two minutes and President Clinton was on the phone. The Queen briefly spoke to him and handed the phone to Dad.

President Clinton said, "Hello, your Majesty. Are things going well? Queen Elizabeth said you wanted to speak to me."

Dad replied, "I want to ride on Air Force One back home. I want to go to my American home. Can you do that for me?"

The President said, "Consider it done. We can't protect you well in your American home, though. I want you to come visit me at the White House to discuss your departure back to the Island of Patmos."

Dad said, "Bye," and handed the phone to the Queen. The Queen had a well- pleased look on her face. She had that look that mom get when she wants to show off her new discovery. She was very dignified about it.

The Queen sat for about a half-hour with dad, chatting. She totally explained everything and answered dad's questions. Dad thought that all those stories grandpa told him about being a king were just stories to make a kid feel good. Grandpa never did act like a dignified king. He was so playful. I always wondered where he lived. He would never let me visit, but I always knew he would come again.

All of those stories I heard as a kid were actually true, mmm. No wonder I act so weird. My friends always said, "Sonthy walks high like she is a princess." Now I know I really am a princess. Mmm, that didn't mean a thing to me though. It just proved what I knew in my heart all along. I don't need other people to tell me who I am. All I had to do was believe in myself and know who I was. Everything else always fell in place. I just could not believe dad was a king! He acted so stuffy.

Sunday came and mom and dad were on Air Force One going home. Mom told me that the Queen wired one point five billion American dollars into dad's account. This was a present to the king because Queen Elizabeth was happy to have finally found him. Mom said the Queen told her that she felt pretty awful about dad's leg. Mom was very loving about the whole event. That's why I loved my mother. She had to be the greatest mother any body could ever have.

I was in bed with Charles the next day when my phone started ringing. I got off my bed, and answered the phone.

"Hello," I said.

It was mom. She was excited about everything that was going on.

She said, very rapidly, "ajoihauh;iha"

I said, "Mom! Hold on a minute. You know, I think that's where I get that from. When you talk so fast, you just don't make any sense. You sound like shit!"

Mom said. "One point five billion dollars was actually in dad's account! I went the other day to withdraw some money from the bank.... Sally was extra nice to me. You know that witch that everybody hates, the mean lady. I ordered a Mercedes from that lot we always passed by on the way home from church. They brought it to me at the bank within ten minutes! Can you believe that? Guess who was driving. Sally's husband, Fred. You know how he was. Even his own voice is scared of him. He's the guy that used to make fun of me when I was small..., and..., and..."

I stopped her, cause she would have just wheedled my ears off. It would have been a long time before I could have persuaded my ear to get back on my head.

One time she spoke to me for five hours straight on the phone without me saying a word. She was so excited. She was telling me about all the poems she wrote about me. She really loved the one she wrote when I was born. She had to break each poem down and tell me what each word meant to her. I loved her so much, but when five hours passed by on the phone and my ear was red and had not seen sunshine since Santa Claus was born, that's when I had to sorrowfully and regretfully tell my mom, "Mom, my ear hurts. I think it's bleeding. There is blood all over the kitchen tile. It was dripping everywhere and the aliens are oozing out my head through that ear!" I didn't want to pull another alien oozing thing, so I just stopped her, cause it always made me feel bad when I had to exaggerate to my mommy. But she was really cute, though.

I could just see her at that moment. Her blonde hair, mixed with grey, tied up in a bun. Her round, red cheeks flushed even brighter as her excitement would build. When she got really excited, her whole body would shake like a giant Jell-O mold. That's when I would give her a big hug. I always gave her a hug when she was really excited. For Pete's sake, I would have too! She never took a breath. I would have to hug her so she would breath! Sometimes, I loved her so much, I used to get sick if she left the room. That only happened until I was sixteen; then boys took over.

Then, I got sick when I saw some boy who was really good looking. When boys looked that good, all I could can compare them with was food, because I loved food, too. Food always looked good to me! Even after I was finished eating. I usually took a second helping just because it tasted so good! Food would always taste good to me. When boys started looking as good as food, that's when my body would get confused!

Anyway, mom called just to share some of her excitement, even though she interrupted a few excitements of my own with Charles. See, that was the way it was. Now that I had had sex, I would get a little confused whether food is better or sex is better. But, if I really had to choose between them both, I would have to negotiate and only eat one helping of my favorite dish, along with only one helping of an orgasm, instead of multiple helpings of food and orgasms!

Mom said, "Good bye."

I said, "Tell your Majesty that I still love him. He is still my 'Computer Norby.' Bye." I hung up the phone.

I returned to my sinful pleasures. Where was I?... Oh yeah. I was sitting on that hard thing handsomely poking up, and ... the phone rang again.

Charles told me not to answer it, but I did anyways. I regretted answering it. It was the Zum Man. Talk about making me feel like puking. Every time I would hear his voice, I would think of a giant King Cobra, swallowing whole adults. What a viper! I pleasantly answered the phone in my sweetest, innocent voice. I thought that it could be mom again. Maybe she forgot to tell me something. The Zum Man said, "The lobby. Six o'clock sharp."

Well, that voice quenched my sex drive. I had to tell Charles that it was time to pack. He helped me packed. Then, it was morning.

Charles caught the eleven o'clock flight, but, as for me, well... I had the unpleasant task of smelling Mr. Zum's royal "ball head-ness" on a helicopter ride to some remote island north of Great Britain. Off I went to begin my new career in genetic engineering.

Chapter 3

The Twins

The twins were born on April first, nineteen fifty-nine, at midnight. They both had bright blonde hair and green eyes. They were the cutest things you ever did see. They were chunky, though. The Hennepin County Medical Center in downtown Minneapolis was just as packed as ever that night.

Their parents, Caroline and Dave Johnson, were a handsome couple. Caroline was swearing and sweating during the delivery. Her legs were propped up on the stirrups. Her hair was sticky. Her face had tears of sweat slowly crawling down her cheeks like some amphibious reptile. Her cheeks were bright red. Her stomach was so big the doctor could only see half of her face when she was pushing. She was wearing one of those blue hospital gowns. It was the kind that you had to tie in the back. She was determined as hell to have babies. It took ten hours for the first one to come out. She did real fine when the first son popped out. He came rushing out like a pink balloon jerking to the surface of the swimming pool. After all that effort, the wind went out of her sail.

Carol and Dave were both resident doctors at HCMC. Dave worked in OB/GYN and Caroline worked in the Emergency Room. They had been dating for eight years when they first met as freshmen at the University of Minnesota. They both did their internships at Mayo Clinic in Rochester. They felt very lucky to have both ended up doing their residency at Hennepin County Medical Center.

It was definitely convenient to have the baby while she was working. The contractions had just started after she checked out her first patient. David was upstairs in OB/GYN, delivering babies, when he got called to his wife's delivery. David wasn't allowed to deliver his own babies, though.

Like I said before, she was praying and determined those first ten hours, until she found out she was having twins. Then, the wind went right out of her. Carol said, "It's all your fault, Dave. If you didn't have such a fucking long penis, all those sperm wouldn't have been up there!"

Dave replied, "Try to push, Honey."

"Push my fucking ass! You try to deliver two ten-pound watermelons through your penis. Don't tell me to push! It hurts so bad, Honey, help me! Isn't there … uh, huh, Oooh it's coming! It's coming!" She yelled. Two minutes later, the other pink boy popped to the top of the swimming pool and started crying. Dave's eyes were huge. He was so amazed. He had seen many deliveries before, but these were the only ones that looked exactly like him. Dave was very proud.

Carol and Dave had a very good relationship. They were best friends when they got married. They had been married one year, and now they were having a family. Neither one of them knew anything about parenting, but they did plenty of reading on it.

They brought their babies, Devin and Dylan, home to twelve fifty-five Russell Avenue. The two children were opposite in temperament. Devin, the oldest by one minute, was the feistiest and most aggressive. He was known as the "crazy one." Dylan was extremely easy in temperament. He was the thinker. Devin just acted on whatever feeling he had.

Their house was a small, split-level two-bedroom. It was cream in color with red trimming around the windows. It was on a little hill on the East Side of Plymouth. Penn and Plymouth intersected a few blocks north of their house. The East Side of Plymouth was where the rich people lived. It was where the golf course and the ski jumps were. It had a creek running through the center of the golf course.

But, on the West Side, there was a whole lot of Negro folks. They weren't as educated, like my friend Charles. These people were the kind that sat on their porches all day. The men, the children and the women didn't do much. They just hung out most of the day, until the Brotherhood gang sprayed machine gun bullets through their windows, which happened quite frequently. The Brotherhood owned the West Side. They were always fighting with the other gangs over territory, drugs, prostitution and weaponry. The police never got involved, as long as the gangs didn't cross over to the wealthier and more prominent East Side. Carol and David weren't aware of these activities, whatsoever. They were too busy being doctors.

Their kids went to Mother Theresa's private Catholic school until their senior year. They convinced Dave and Carol that all their friends went to Central. Besides, they were tired of all that religious stuff. Their parents were not even Catholic. They didn't have a religion except Monday night football. Finally Dave and Carol told them if they got good grades, they could attend Central High School their last year. Central High School was the toughest school in North Minneapolis. Usually someone was killed once every six months there. Most teachers survived by being parents of a gang member, or adopting gang activities as part of their family.

Dylan and Devin did well at Central. They both graduated with straight A's and went to college. They were very bright young men. The twins got involved in gang activities, simply because Dave and Carol were not around to be involved in their lives. The Brotherhood gang provided the attention and belonging that teenage boys craved. The two boys found respect and power in this gang.

They were tired of being "Dr. Johnson's kids." Every circle they were in, they were always "Dr. Johnson's kids." Devin and Dylan hated being "Dr. Johnson's kids." They thought, "How the hell could a man be a kid?" Dave and Carol didn't know that they had already killed six people. Kids don't kill that many people!

The whole time that they were in college, they had a silent rebellion. When they both graduated with their master's, their parents were proud. Devin got his master in genetic engineering, and Dylan received his in business administration. Little did the parents know how much education their children really received over the past seven years. The boys wanted to make money and still be young. They didn't want any of this retirement shit!

Devin and Dylan got involved in the Brotherhood gang immediately after going to Central. They both became real good friends with the Zum Man. The Zum Man was very powerful in the Brotherhood because he killed like a machine: systematically and without feelings. The Zum Man had to initiate the two brothers when they entered the gang. Each of them had to kill three people. So, the Zum Man taught Devin and Dylan his favorite way of killing his people.

The Zum Man said to Devin and Dylan, "I take pride in killing the biggest and meanest dude. A warrior is not courageous if he can't kill his strongest opponent. First thing I would do is to create a strategy. My favorite one was I would hire the prettiest prostitute and take her to a night club. I would have her sit at a table by herself. I would make sure it was a table that was in front where every man passing by could see her cleavage."

The Zum Man would pause and laugh. I hated that laugh. He laughed like he did that night at the dinner table when I lost my appetite. He took in a deep, long breath. Then, he held it for a couple of seconds while he tucked in his chin and wrinkled his eyebrows downward in the center. Finally, he would smile with all those white teeth and let out the deepest, huskiest ha-ha's. I hated those laughs. I didn't know what it was about, that Zum Man, but he took too much pleasure in those stories!

The Zum Man continued. He was very excited. The veins in his neck looked like they were going to burst. They became large and puffy and he said, "I would sit a couple of tables from the Bitch, then I waited. If a guy was on her at her table that I thought wasn't big enough, or wasn't threatening, I would walk over to the table and intimidate the hell out of the Son of a Bitch. But if a good size penis came, then it was time to kill!"

Zum Man paused and continued, "I would have the lady get a hotel and fuck him all night until he was good and tired. I would be in the closet the whole time. When he was tired, I came out of the closet with my gun. I would get his fucking white ass off the Bitch and sit him naked on a chair facing the woman. I would have the woman tie his arms and legs and then tie him to the chair. Then I would sit next to the woman and tell the Son of a Bitch how I was going to kill him with the hammer in my hand."

"Before I killed him," The Zum man stammered on, "I'd have the Bitch shave his head bald, just like mine. I made sure he understood that I thought he was a worthless piece of slime. If he was married and had a ring on his finger, I would just cut off his penis. While he was screaming, I'd tell the Whore to kiss him. In the middle of them kissing, I would slowly walk behind him and smash his head until white brain matter and blood sprayed all over the Bitch! Then I'd give her the money and tell her to clean her fucking ass. Then I would tell the Bitch she was mine for the rest of her life. If she was good, I would keep her, but when she began annoying me, I would shove my gun in her mouth and blow her brains out!"

In this manner, Devin and Dylan became expert killers. Soon, they became powerful, by killing certain government officials and using fear to intimidate officials in order to manipulate the drug cartel. That was how they brought millions into the Brotherhood gang. Life and death, they thought, was a great way to persuade officials.

They became instrumental in bringing military arms to the streets. Everybody in the Brotherhood gang thought Devin was crazy because he, like the Zum man loved to kill. But Dylan, on the other hand, loved business. The gang feared and respected them both as their leaders, even the Zum Man.

Dylan talked Devin into making the Brotherhood a company and now it was called "The Brotherhood, Inc." Dylan and Devin organized the gang and made it a proficient system. The company dealt in drugs, weapons, prostitution, and human cloning, genetic research, but most of all, organ production and transplants. Most of the money the company received from drugs, weapons, and prostitution was funneled into organ production and transplants through genetic engineering. The company dumped millions into organ reproduction. They had three hundred categories of organ warehouses on thousands of acres. These warehouses were full of human organs that were grown in the laboratory and sold through the black market. They professed their company to be a genetic engineering research firm. I had never seen such a large scaled genetic cloning in all my life! It took me a while to figure out why I was hired. It was to keep those warehouses full of human organs.

It was Devin's idea to do genetic reproduction and research. This was how he stumbled on the idea. One, day he was having a discussion with a policeman about his BMW being stripped and torn apart. Devin came from a meeting and saw his Beamer's frame sitting next to the curb. He could see right through it. There were no seats, steering wheel, dashboard, tires, hood, or engine. All that was left was simply the housing. At first Devin was thinking whom he could kill for doing this, but then an idea popped in his mind. He asked the cop, "Why did they strip my car?"

The policeman answered, "To sell the parts."

From that point on, Devin kept thinking about selling body parts during the entire taxi ride to the office. Once he arrived back to his own office, he wanted a meeting with Dylan to discuss his new ideas.

On the way up to discuss these ideas with Dylan, Devin entered the elevator and pushed the fiftieth floor button with his index finger. Their office was on the fiftieth floor of the IDS Tower in downtown Minneapolis. He was deep in thought when the elevator's bell sounded to remind him that he was on his floor. Stepping out of the elevator, he noticed the surrounding glass walls. They both had bean-shaped glass desks placed next to each other tucked in the north east corner of the glass office. The desks were facing the large double glass doors entering the office. They had curtains that covered the glass wall between their receptionist and their office.

That day Dylan was dressed in his usual black, pinstriped, three-piece suit. His jacket was hanging on the wall over on the rack. He was sitting on a white leather sofa, facing the windows. His neatly pressed white sleeve of his shirt followed his arm that led to his hand, poised on his chin. His legs were crossed neatly, in a fashion that showed his calm demeanor. Dylan stared out the large glass windows while he listened. Devin on the other hand, was walking back and forth in front of the light streamed windows. Devin didn't like three piece suits, but he gladly wore his coat and tie. He was wearing a white sports coat, a white shirt, and a gold silk tie.

Devin was excited about his plans. He tilted his head backward and sighed. He reached in the air, as if he was reaching through a window. He grabbed an invisible fruit out of the air and said, "Look Dylan, the harvest is ready."

Dylan didn't budge an eye. He was used to Devin's dramatic style. Devin continued, "First we will get the best of our employees to mate and produce children, like the Catholic Church. Second, we will take eggs from the woman and sperm from the men to create our own immortal children. We will eradicate all mortal man through a genetic virus. We will set our immortal child to repopulate the earth. We will be the rulers of the whole earth over our genetic immortals. We will be as gods and live forever. Third, we will use the children's DNA to clone twins like us. Fourth, when the cloned children become old enough, we will put them under anesthesia and gut them out and take their parts and store them to sell, while they grow new organs.

These people will be cloned individuals and won't have birth certificates. We will produce them like GMC manufactured cars. When we need new gene pools, we'll hire more employees. We already have the human genetic map, let's make some damn money! Finally, we can grow and produce new and non-diseased organs fresh and ready for transplant. We will spread this virus through the transplants. All we have to do is keep them in warehouses. It's just like producing a 'human junkyard.' We remove the parts out of the clones and use them for other humans. What do you think of my idea Dylan?"

Dylan thought for a long time. He didn't say a word for ten minutes. After a while, he finally spoke slowly. He said, "We have to work out the logistics."

"Well, of course. You can't call them real people anyway. We won't give them names. It would be like a prison for them. They won't know any other world!" Devin said. Devin's eyes were getting excited.

Dylan interrupted, "The employees that are having babies will have to have family units, but not be actual families. We'll have to have our own hospital, too. We could create a psychiatric hospital and drug the clones up just enough so they'll eat, drink, and shit! And last of all, we'll have to have a burial ground and a crematorium."

Devin loudly interjected, "Hell yea! We could even clone certain important world leaders, and provide organs for them when needed. But what I like the best is, we could even replace those world leaders with clones and no one would know it. Remember that movie we watched....what was it called?"

Dylan said, "It was called *The Replacement*. I liked the part when they finally shot the real president and nobody knew that the replacement was a clone."

Devin yelled, "Helleluyah my brother! I think you've got the vision! The fields are ready for harvest! We could have our own replacement. Shit! We will replace the whole fucking human race!"

Then Dylan quickly stood up and started pacing. When Dylan started pacing, you knew it was a done deal. He was working out all the logistics.

Dylan pushed the button on the phone. "Yes sir," said Martha, their Executive Secretary.

"Call a Corporate Executive General assembly in five days. Make it the first thing Monday morning, eight o'clock. Nobody will be late. Anyone who is late will be shot on the spot. Devin and I will be in here for the next five days. You will be, too.

Bring us some food every eight hours. Martha, get Mr. Zum's ass in here. Call him on his cell phone!"

"Yes sir," she said. She quickly dialed his number. The phone rang.

He answered, "Speak!"

"Moocher 3… Moocher 1 and Moocher 2 want you in their office, Code Blue." The Zum Man always answers his cell phone with his famous command, "Speak!" What the hell, he's so primal. That's probably why I didn't like him. I wished I knew what role he played in this Corporation. I'm still trying to pin point him. I never did find out what Moocher 1, 2, 3 meant.

Monday came fast. There were cars squealing into the parking ramps. The corporate conference room was full. The Terminator was there, "The Man in the Mask." Devin was calmly watching his watch. He said, "Time's up! Close the doors." The Masked Man closed the large, glass double doors. Just as he was closing them, our newest corporate attorney, Mr. Deable came running in. He had been with the company for a year. He was always late. He came in, pushing on the doors, while the Terminator was shutting them.

Suddenly, the Masked Man yanked him inside by his suit and slammed him face up on the long glass conference table. Everybody suddenly backed away from the table. Nobody got out of his or her chair. The Masked Man jumped on top of Mr. Deables's belly and immediately whipped out a needle and a syringe and jabbed the needle into his white eyeball. You heard a loud pop! Immediately, the corrosive chemical blew out his eye.

The Masked Man stood him up on the ground and let him go. Mr. Deables was screaming and going in circles grabbing his eye. There were white strands of eye ligaments dangling between his fingers. They were mixed with blood and green chemical stuff. He was yelling, "Aahh, noooo, my eye, my eye, my -."

The silencer on the gun went off right in his chest and he fell down. The Masked Man slowly put his gun down. He walked over to the man and then slowly walked over to a corner and stood there.

Devin got up and walked over to the Masked Man, got his gun, took the silencer off, and emptied the rest of the bullets into Mr. Deables's head, splattering fragments across the floor. Then, when he was finished, he went to his desk and pushed the phone button. He slowly said, "Martha, call the Eraser and get this piece of shit off my floor."

When he was finished, he gave the gun back to the Masked Man and took his seat. Dylan stood up and said, "Ladies and gentlemen, I call this meeting to order. We will be expanding our operation."

Chapter 4

My Associate

I had been working for The Brootherhood, Inc. for one year. They had given me a house on their compound. The house was a three-bedroom ranch style dwelling. It was very nice. It was rustic on the outside. It had a deck that went completely around the house. The house was built on a lake. I had a long dock that had a supercharged company boat. Sometimes I would take the boat out and fly across the lake like it had wings. I did not have any visitors from the outside of the corporation since I had been here. I had been so busy at work that when I got home, I would just veg out or work on my Sister Earth project.

Many times, I would call to talk to dad or mom. Mom and dad don't live together anymore. Mom didn't want to leave the US. Dad had to leave her home. So we had two homes. Mom would fly back and forth to see dad. She was happy dad was gone. She got to play more without him throwing one of his emotional fits.

When my phone would ring, I would answer it with "The Son." Not like the Sun as in sunshine, but the Son as in Son of the Father. What's really interesting about this company is everyone had to have a name other than their own. You either picked a name to be called, or they pick one for you. I picked "The Son." Son was the closest to Sonthy that I could find, so when mom or dad called, I pick up the phone and said, "The Son." Mom and dad asked me why I answer the phone like that and I just explained to them that it was short for Sonthy. Mom said she kinda liked it. Dad just grumbled. When mom would call and I'd answer "The Son," She would say, "Shining Bright!"

The phone rang. I picked it up. "The Son."

"Shining Bright," a woman said on the other end.

I yelled, "Mom! Hi mom! I miss you. When do I get to see you again?"

"Well, when do you get vacation time dear? I'll come visit," She said.

"I don't know. I have to ask the Zum Man. I'll get back to you. Mom, I'm very tired. It's been a long day. Can I call you this weekend? I think I want to go to bed."

"Okay, Dear," she said. We said our good-byes and I hung up the phone.

Actually, my phone was in the shape of a black penis that I ordered out of a magazine. I just punched the number keys right on the balls. I always thought about getting me some every time I picked up the phone. It reminded me of Charles. I was actually feeling some powerful emotions about Charles. I hadn't seen him for a year, but we e-mailed each other everyday since I had been at my new place. I didn't think I would e-mail him that night, though. I was really tired.

I started to get ready for bed. I went into the bathroom. I took a shower, put on my white, silky pajamas, and hopped in bed. I laid down that night and fell into an unusually deep sleep. I had four dreams that I remembered. The first one was about a Volkswagen Beetle (one of the newer models), being chased by a big black Monster Truck. It said, 'BHI' Killer Machine on the side of it. The windows were tinted and you couldn't see the driver in the truck. I saw another vehicle. It was an earthmover. It was so big. I never saw anything that big in my life! The tires were huge! It was chasing the Monster Truck, which was chasing the Beetle.

There was an invisible crane that hoisted the Beetle into the air. In the middle of the air, there was a large cloud, shaped into a fist. The index finger pointed straight up. There was a garage sitting above the clouds where the index finger was pointing. Written on the garage it said, "Sister Earth." The invisible crane lifted the Beetle into the garage. The Beetle disappeared as it entered the garage and the door closed. The Monster Truck ran out of gas and stopped. The slow-moving earthmover saw the Monster Truck, but ran over it anyway. The Monster Truck went underneath it and was crushed like an aluminum can.

In the second dream, I saw a caterpillar attached to a leaf that went into a cocoon. The cocoon hatched; a pretty yellow butterfly flew out. There was a Grim Reaper with a sickle in his right hand. On the blade of the sickle, it had the initials BHI. In the left hand, the Grim Reaper had a butterfly net. A strong wind came that blew the Grim Reaper into the path of an "F-five" tornado. The Grim Reaper was destroyed. The strong wind shifted its disposition and dissipated. A large, radiant rainbow ran right into the sunshine. At the end of the running, righteous rainbow there was a pot of gold. The pot itself was made out of glimmering golden glory. In the glorious gold, there was a sign that said, "S.E." The yellow butterfly landed on the sign, then looked down and saw thousands of different colored butterflies playing in the glorious gold.

In my third dream there was a beautiful billowing, bright white pillar of cloud. There was a giant hurricane that wanted to consume the pretty planted pillar. The cool, cushiony, cloudy, white mass didn't move or hurt anybody. It was a peaceful, polite, pretty pillar. The hurricane roughly raged to rapidly run right through the pillar, but when it came to shore, it dissipated. Soon, there was no hurricane. After the hurricane evaporated, a hummingbird came out of the white, cloudy pillar. The hummingbird flew to a yellow trumpet-shaped flower that was as big as the Sears Tower. The flower was sitting in a large flowerpot that said, "S.E." on it. When the humbled humming bird saw the large, yellow flower, it dove into the center of it to eat some nectar. Behold, in the middle of the flower were thousands of other hiding, humbled humming birds eating nectar, too!

In the fourth dream, I saw an angel come down from heaven with a torch in his right hand. His assignment was to burn down a large statue that cast it's shadow over the whole earth. On the base of the statue, there was a sign that said, "BHI." I heard a large, explosive noise below me. When I looked down, I saw hell open her mouth. I saw large, lazy, crackling flames leaping out of the deep, dark, dungeon. The smoking abyss brought fourth a reptilian lizard that had two heads. It was the giant dragon of old. Leviathan was his name. He had two long tongues, with slits at the end of them, coming out of his mouths. Then he stuck his tongues out, like a frog swallowing flies from the air. The two tongues swept hundreds of men, women, and children into his mouths and ate them. I saw the flesh, limbs, torsos, and heads rolling around in his mouths and being crushed by those long, white iron claws called teeth. The beast threw his tongues around the angel's waist and tried to place the angel in his mouths, but the angel burned the beast's tongues with his torch. The beast made a loud hissing roar that caused an earthquake. The earthquake caused a large water fountain to spray out of the ground, to form a rushing, mighty river. The fountain spray knocked the beast out of the sky. The thing came crashing down into the river. The violent river washed the beast into the sea and it drowned. There was a battle ship in the water that scooped the dead beast up out of the water. The men ground up the beast into fish food and dumped it back into the Ocean. The angel lit up the statue into flames, and the battle ship used its guns to blow the statue into bits. I heard the sailors on the ship celebrate with shouting. They began to ring the ship's bell.

I woke up to the ringing of the phone, thinking it was the ship's bell. I slowly opened my eyes. I glanced at the digital clock. It was five-thirty in the morning. I wondered who could be calling me so early. Give me a little respect. I'm going to kill them, I thought. I picked up the cordless on the nightstand by my bed.

"The Son," I answered.

"Get your things packed. The driver will take you to the helicopter. You will be going to Minneapolis, Minnesota. You are reassigned. When you get there, I will call you." He hung up. It was the Zum Man. I just didn't like his voice. He had not even given me a chance to ask about my vacation! Well, I was going to Minneapolis anyway. That Zum Man was getting on my nerves.

The driver got me to the helicopter on time. My luggage and items were sent to Minneapolis. It was delivered by a moving van to the house. They had a nice big, white house completely furnished with white beautiful furniture. They even had a white grand piano. I wondered what was the obsession with white? The house was in New Brighton, Minnesota. You go north on Long Lake Road until you hit Irondale High School. You take a right on Poppyseed. Follow Poppyseed until you get to the end. The road will continue to the right. Follow it until you get to a big, white house on the left. You know, the one that has brown doors and brown trimming. The only split-level, white house from the corner.

The house was pretty neat. It had a two-car garage in the front. Then there was a driveway that went along side of the house. The driveway went down a hill behind the house. Underneath the first two-car garage, there was another two-car garage. In the first two-car garage, there was a large, silver fire pole. It looked like a pole fireman slid down to get to the ground level.

The master bedroom was upstairs. It was shaped into a giant "L." The long part of the "L" was facing east and the short part was facing north. The north section of the "L" was the master bathroom. Right before you would head into the bathroom on your left, there was a light brown wooden door. The door opened outward onto a little tiny patio that had handrails on sides. On the front was the large, round silver pole.

In the morning, when I was in a rush, I would push the garage door opener on the wall to my left. The opener looked like a doorbell. It was on the inside of the house. When I was in a rush, I would push it, and then leap on the fire pole and slide down to the first floor. I landed right next to my Mitsubishi 3000 GT. Then, I was gone.

There was a little bedroom attached to the northeast side, next to the master bathroom. The little bedroom had an indoor little deck that looked down into the living room.

The master bedroom was really sweet. The bedroom itself had sliding glass patio doors, leading to an outside deck. The deck faced the backyard. The backyard was about fifty yards. It was shaped into an arrow.

Long Lake and Rice Creek met at a right angle behind the house. The tip of the arrow was the right angle. Sometimes I got a boat to be alone, and get away from my roommate.

The master bedroom also had it's own inner living room, or den. That's where I spent most of my time. The den had an outside and inside patio. Except, the inside patio didn't have sliding glass doors like the outside one did. When you looked over the inside patio, you looked right into the living room.

The living room had a high, vaulted ceiling. I remember how I would look down on my associate playing the piano. My associate was to be my roommate. He was to work with me, but I'll tell you about that later.

The dining room was on the first floor underneath the den. The kitchen was attached to the back wall of the house. If you looked through the kitchen windows, you could see the back yard.

To enter the house in the front, you had to go through these large brown double doors. But first there was a funny looking porch. The porch had large railroad ties that were attached to the house in a perpendicular fashion. There were about ten of them parallel to each other. The beams had ten inches of space between them. There were three vertical beams holding up all the other horizontal and parallel beams.

Downstairs, below the ground level, was another bedroom. The stairway was between the living room and the kitchen that led downstairs. There was a queen-size bed that hung on chains from the ceiling in the lower bedroom. As you came down the stairs the bedroom was on your left. On your right you had the living area and another sliding patio door. The whole floor was artificial turf. There were golf holes in the floor. If you wanted to practice your golf, all you had to do was open the holes and stick some flags in them.

There was a waterfall high up on the east wall that was three feet wide. The waterfall came to the floor and turned into an indoor creek three feet wide that flowed to the west wall. When you walked out of the lower bedroom, you would walk about fifteen feet on the artificial turf to a wooden bridge with handrails. This first bridge would lead to the first patio and sliding glass doors. The creek continued to flow westward and a second little waterfall three feet wide and two feet high would soon appear. The floor sank one level down and the turf continued. Four feet after the waterfall there was another brown wooden bridge with side-rails that lead to another patio and sliding glass doors. The creek continued about two feet after the bridge, into a small pool that re-circulated to the waterfall. The house that the Brotherhood, Inc. assigned to me was a winner. I was very proud to be living here.

The phone rang. I answered, "The Son."

It was the Zum Man. He said, "I'll be over in fifteen minutes to introduce you to your new associate. He will be your roommate. Order some Chinese food. I'll do chicken, he'll do shrimp. We will eat dinner when we get there." He hung up.

What! Was he born in a zoo? He couldn't even say hello or goodbye? He would not let anyone speak after he talked! He had to hang up the dumb phone! I would just start to open my mouth to speak and he would hang up. I was getting sick and tired of his lack of professional courtesy! We worked for the same damn company! I was beginning to really hate that Zum shit! The whole time I was speaking to myself, I was pacing back and forth, grasping my left hand in a tight fist and shaking my index finger at God. I was furious! Mom always said, "If a man don't have manners, he ain't got no love inside him, except hate."

I shook my finger at God again and said, "I think Mr. Zum is pure rude. One day I'm going to slap some fucking manners into him!"

I left a window open earlier. In the middle of cussing, a fly flew in my mouth. I gasped for air, hacking and coughing. I shook my finger at God again and said, "Okay, I get the point.

Quit feeding me flies. I'm going to eat Chinese fried shrimp pretty soon."

I went to the kitchen, pulled up a barstool next to the phone and sat down at the kitchen counter. I dialed Mom's number. The phone rang a couple of times, mom picked it up.

She answered, "The Savitri's."

"Hi mom. It's me. Guess what?" I said.

"What Dear?" She said.

"Mom, I'm here in the states. I'm only in New Brighton, off Poppyseed road. It's that house that we use to drive by and wonder what it's like inside. I'm living in it now. It's really beautiful. Do you want to come over for dinner? Oh, by the way, the Zum Man is coming with my associate. I'm supposed to work with some guy. He'll be my roommate."

Mom listened quietly. I knew what she was thinking. She was thinking that living with a guy is not morally ethical. Of course she thought that it was my new guy. But I would have to set her straight when she came. She hesitantly replied, "Honey I don't like that bald headed man. But for you, I'll be right there. See you in ten. Bye, Dear."

"Thanks mom, you're the best. Bye." I hung up.

The doorbell rang. I thought to myself, it's Scum Man. I opened the door very slowly. There he was, just like I thought, Scum Man in the flesh. I barely opened the door and Scumbag walked right through. I quickly moved back so he didn't run into me.

He said, "Where's the food?"

I said, "It hasn't come yet." The door was still wide open. There was a very handsome man with him. He was tall. I bet he was about six foot-two inches. He had beautiful, shiny jet-black hair that was neatly groomed. He had shinning, clear, blue eyes. His mustache was neatly trimmed. A brief, nasty thought came into my head about his mustache. I quickly brushed it aside. It was a very good thought, though. Ouch, he was hot! He looked like Clark Gable. He had a flowing, square face that was smooth in its complexion. When he smiled, he had those soft long dimples. He was dressed in a white three-piece suit with white shoes.

What was it with white? Inside the whole house was white and now this guy shows up in white. The only thing I liked about Mr. Scumbag was that he... at least wore a black pinstriped. I was wearing my blue summer dress that had lace around the bottom.

Mr. Scumbag went into the living room and sat down on the white leather sofa. The handsome, polite gentleman just followed him and sat across from him on the plush, white leather chair. I sat on the love seat. My hair was up. I suddenly had this strong impulse to let it down. So I took my hair clip out and slowly pushed my glossy, blonde hair back behind my shoulders.

I glanced over at the young man. He was about my age. He politely smiled and nodded his head. Oooo, I loved those dimples! I felt my appetite suddenly kick in. I caught myself staring at the stranger.

I faintly heard someone call my name. "The Son." I didn't answer. He spoke up a little louder. "The Son! Are you with us? Will you get the door? Didn't you here the door bell ring?" said the Zum Man.

"Oh, I'm sorry. I was thinking." I got up and answered the door.

"Hi Mom!" I let her in and gave her a big hug. There was a guy standing behind her with a bunch of bags. Mom and I helped him with the food. I gave him a five-dollar tip and closed the door behind him.

Mom and I walked over to the kitchen and sat the food on the counter. Mom got out the dishes and set the table. I took the food out of the bags. When I was finished, I went to the living room. When I got there I said, "Gentlemen, the food is ready. Will you join us?"

They both got up. Mr. Zum Man led the way. He sat at the head of the table on the West Side. Mom sat opposite of him on the East Side. I sat on the South Side with my back towards the backyard. My associate sat directly opposite of me. Mr. Zum Man said to Mom, "This is R.W.."

Then he looked at me and said, "This is your associate, R.W.. R.W., this is Mrs. Savitry and your associate, The Son."

The polite gentleman backed his chair out, walked over to mom, shook her hand and said in a deep and distinct voice, "It is a pleasure to meet you." Then he walked around the table to me and said, "It's going to be a pleasure working with you." I didn't look at him. I just put out my hand and he shook it with both of his hands. With his right hand he grabbed mine, and with his left hand, he slowly cup my hand inside his. He left his index finger to slowly caress my skin as he spoke. His big hand felt deliciously warm. He gently squeezed my hand and I got slow-oozing, warm tingles through my entire body. They went up my neck and through my fingertips. I took a deep breath and quickly started eating. R.W. sat down and began to eat.

Mom was bubbly and chatty as usual. Thank God she was there. She broke the silence. She said to the Zum Man, "Do you like Europe as much as I do?"

The Zum Man replied, "I would love Europe if you were there with me."

Mom said, "Are you frisking me, young man?"

The Zum Man said, "I'm working on it."

I rolled my eyes at Zum Bag. I kicked Mom under the table. Mom shouldn't flirt with an ugly man like that. R.W. just sat there and watched me intensely. He knew something about me. I wondered what it was. He treated my mom like he knew her. After a long silent time, R.W. said to mom. "It's been a long time since I've seen you. It's good to see you again."

Mom said, "Oh, I don't remember you."

R.W. replied, "It was a long time ago."

Mom said, "Mmmm, you don't seem that old to me."

He said, "Well, it's like seeing a movie, you forget the characters if you don't see it again."

I jumped in the conversation and said, "Did you see *Nine Millimeters* with Nicolas Cage? I saw it in Europe. I thought he had inspirational courage, but I thought it was dumb."

Mr. Zum interjected, "Why do you think it's dumb?"

I squinted my eyes as I buried them down his dark spirit. I forcefully replied, "The fat man in the mask that went around killing innocent girls was a weak man. He can't go face to face with someone who's able to fight back. He has to pick someone who's helpless, then tie her up. On top of it all, he doesn't have the guts to show his face. He has to always wear a mask. Only killers that are afraid of being killed wear masks. He has to wear a mask because he is weak!"

The Zum Man replied, "So you think you know a lot about killers?"

I quickly interjected, "I didn't say I knew a lot about all killers, I said that particular killer is weak. Why would a warrior kill a weak enemy, theirs no victory in it!"

The Zum Man took a deep breath, then said, "Killers like him don't kill because they want sweet victory. Killers like that kill because they want to, and it gives them pleasure to kill."

I was watching mom, she didn't like this subject. She was getting uncomfortable. I knew my Mom. She liked beautiful topics. Like the movies, *The Sound of Music*, or *Willy Wonka and the Chocolate Factory*. She also liked *Chitty, Chitty, Bang Bang*. Her all time favorite movie was *E.T.*. Mom slid her chair back and quickly stood up. The men stood up with her. I found myself sitting alone.

Mom said, "It's getting late, I need to sleep Dear. I'll call you."

I stood up, she gave me a hug and I walked her to the door. I opened the front door, kissed her on her cheek and watched her drive away in her new, pearl- colored Mercedes. I closed the door.

I turned around and Mr. Scumbag was right behind me! I jumped backwards. I was startled. My back fell against the door. Both my hands were on the doorknob still. Oh, how I hated him!

He just got on my nerves. He said, "I'll see you later. Would you excuse me?"

I opened the door for him. As he walked out, he slowly turned his big bald head to his left and stared at me. He had that evil, angry look. At that moment, fear gripped my body. I quickly closed the door behind him. Something was very eerie about him today.

I quietly walked back to the table. R.W. sat by himself, gently eating his food. I thought he was so handsome, sitting there with his calm demeanor. "I'll help you clean up," he said. His politeness was refreshing. I quickly forgot that Mr. Zum ever existed. R.W. helped me do the dishes. Periodically, I would make some quick glances at him.

I said. "I like a man that's not afraid of getting his fingers wet." He turned, and looked at me. Our eyes caught each other's glance. He grinned, then without saying a word, he went back to doing the dishes. I was burning to ask him a question. I wanted to ask him how he knew my mother, but I never did.

It was about nine o'clock. We just finished the dishes. I helped him unloaded his car. We brought his stuff downstairs in the lower bedroom. Something told me he would be a great roommate. Besides, he's the handsomest roommate I had ever had. When I was done helping R.W., I went upstairs to my room. He politely thanked me with a kiss on my left hand. He had soft lips. His smell was erotic. I started to get goose bumps again. I blushed a little. I left and went to my room. When I got upstairs, I quickly e-mailed my dad and Charles. I had to let them know where I was. I was excited about coming back to the States! Maybe I could get some noogie from Charles. I wanted him to visit this weekend. He was on the computer when I got to mine, so we chatted for a while. I washed up and hit the pillow.

Monday morning came quickly. R.W. worked in management. I didn't know exactly what he did. We drove together, in my car, to work. He showed me around the laboratory where I would be working. He brought me to his office and showed me around. His office was the cleanest place I had ever seen. This guys too clean. Maybe he was gay.

I was very attracted to him, but my mind was in denial. My body was thirsty and hungry. Ever since he came around all I had been thinking was sex. I couldn't let him even get a whiff of it. If he knew I was attracted to him, he might take advantage of our living situation. I didn't think he was that kind of a guy, but I still couldn't take the chance. I had a fleeting thought. Charles was going to come over this weekend and relieve a year of pent-up sexual pressure.

Back to reality, R.W. and I had lunch together at the House of China. He was so charming and funny. He made it easy to talk to him. He had to have some bad in him, some deep, dark secret.

I liked my job. All I was responsible for was taking the samples that they gave me and creating new organs. That was my easiest task, yet. That day I created fifty beating hearts, seventy-five lungs, one hundred pair of eyes, and a bunch of livers. That was an easy day.

The day went fast. R.W. and I drove back home together. On our way home, we stopped to get gas. R.W. pumped the gas and I went into the store to pay for the gas and get some soft drinks for the house. I went around the corner where the cases of beverages were. I grabbed a case of soda. I lifted it up and turned to walk up the aisle. There was that strange, bum, woman. The same old woman I saw at the airport in La Crosse. What the heck? She was wearing the same clothes, and she smelt the same too! She had that alcohol breath combined with a strong musty, moldy odor. I looked at her and immediately my thoughts went to drinking one of those cans of pop. I really loathed her appearance. She needed to shower.

She said to me, in a soft whispery voice, "Hello, you have some drinks there don't you? You certainly have." Her voice was cracking as she stuck that bony, tiny, crooked left index finger at me. She continued to say, "You look hungry. What soul hungers? Does it eat the fig tree? Curse the fig tree I say!" When she said, "Curse the fig tree," some spit sprayed out at me. I quickly backed up so I wouldn't get sprayed on. I suddenly dropped the pop case that I was holding. I bent down to pick it up. When I got up, I looked for the old lady. I looked to my left and to my right. I even looked at the cash register and out the windows. She wasn't around.

I went to pay for the beverages and the gas. I approached the counter, set the beverages on the counter and gave the cashier the money.

I asked the cashier, "Where did that old lady go that had the white hair and smelt funny. The one that had alcohol breath who was standing kind of tipsy?"

The cashier said, "I didn't see any old lady." He turned to the other employee and asked, "Did you see an old lady?"

The second employee replied, "I didn't see anybody."

I noted it again, said, "Mmmm," and walked out the door. I got in the car and R.W. drove away. As he was driving away, I pulled my cell phone out of my purse.

I called from my cell phone and ordered two-sausage pizzas. The pizza deliveryman was there when we pulled into the driveway. I tipped him and we went inside with our nice, hot pizzas. I was hungry. I wolfed down two pieces of pizza like these were the last ones on earth. Oh, yea. That tasted great! Almost as good as sex. Food and sex were my favorite things to do.

I thought about what that Rag Woman said, "Curse the fig tree!" What fig tree? I think she was probably a little mentally retarded. I'm not sure, but I did not own a fig tree. R.W. slowly took his time eating. He was very disciplined. He was thinking to himself, *I hope she boinks like she eats. I'm just going to have to find out.* R.W. continued to eat his pizza, systemically and methodically. This guy was always calm about everything. One day I was going to have to see if I could get him upset.

After we ate, I helped R.W. clean up. I quickly ran upstairs and changed clothes. When I came down stairs, R.W. was sitting in the living room reading the newspaper. I sat on the other couch across from him with my laptop. I was working on my

Sister Earth project. I plugged my laptop into the wall and downloaded some files for dad. Dad got on the chatline and I chatted with him while I worked. He said mom told him about the conversation that we had over dinner with the Zum Man. Dad told me to stay far away from him. I told him that I hated the man anyway; he got on my nerves.

Dad was way cool. Ever since he became King Savitri, he related better to me. I e-mailed him and told him to set me up a lab. I could grow him a new leg when I came to visit. So, I told him all the equipment that I would need.

R.W. raised one eye, periodically, over his paper. One time, I caught him staring at me. I asked, "What the hell are you staring at!"

He replied, "My we're a little feisty tonight. That's good." He went back to reading his paper. He didn't even answer my question.

I e-mailed Dad and told him about this new associate of mine. I told Dad that I didn't know why they made him my roommate. Why didn't they give me my own house like they did in Europe?

Dad replied, "Have you considered the idea of saving money? Killing two birds with one stone?" Dad is so pragmatic. I would have never thought of that. Dad had to go, so we said our good-byes. R.W. got up and went to bed. I worked on my Sister Earth project until midnight. When I went to bed my sleep was sweet.

The week went by fast. I had to leave straight from work to pick up Charles from the Minneapolis/St. Paul International Airport. R.W. and I took separate cars to work that day. R.W. didn't say a thing when I told him Charles, my boyfriend, was coming to visit. He just looked at me and continued what he was doing. Charles arrived on schedule. I picked him up in my Mitsubishi 3000 GL. Charles got in the car, looked around, ran his hands across the dashboard and enthusiastically whistled, "Nice ride."

I responded, with a "Thank you." Our conversation on the drive home was very pleasant. It got my mind off that Rag Woman.

We got home. I turned the car up the driveway, then I opened my driver's door to step out of the car. I heard some thug noise on the other side of the door. I quickly closed the car door to see what it was that I hit with the door. There she was.... the Rag Woman! She lay there on the concrete as if she was unconscious. I scrambled to her rescue. I reached out to grab her arm, and as I grabbed her arms her eyes abruptly opened. I quickly jumped back against the car door. I was surprisingly startled. After getting my breath back, I said, "Boy I'm glad you're not hurt."

She just lay there and pointed that crooked tiny left index finger at me. Then she said, "The sleeping spirits blow greater than the wind, resurrect the dead!" Her whispering voice penetrated my soul. I didn't quite know what to make of it. The Rag Woman continued, "Does genetic ethics bring immortality? Cast the mountain into the sea!"

I suddenly yelled, "Charles! Charles! Quick come here! Help me pick this old lady off the driveway!"

Charles rushed over. Charles looked down at the spot where I was still pointing and said, "What old woman?"

I looked back down at the spot and she was gone! I thought to myself, nah... couldn't be! I said, "Never mind Charles, I'm just hungry. Let's go inside."

Guess who immediately opened the door as we approached? R.W.. He was quite charming standing there with both arms behind his back. He said to Charles, "May I help you with your luggage?"

"Thank you," Charles said. We brought all of Charles luggage to my bedroom. Charles was very excited to see me. I was excited to see him too, but not as much as he was. I was thinking about R.W.. I wondered why he was so nice. Something had to be wrong with him. Maybe he was gay?

We got everything unloaded. Charles and I went downstairs, holding hands, smooching, and giggling. I felt very loved. Charles always gave me his undivided attention. R.W. was at the kitchen table, reading his newspaper. We sat down next to each other, still holding hands. I thought we would visit with R.W. a little bit before we went gallivanting. We sat there for a couple of minutes while R.W. kept reading his newspaper. Charles and I looked at each other, then waited for R.W.'s cue to talk.

R.W. finally sensed that we were waiting to chat. He slowly placed his newspaper on the kitchen table. He crossed his legs, then sat back in his chair with his hands placed on his knees, one on top of the other. He didn't say a thing. He looked at me. I looked at Charles. Charles looked at him, then looked at me. We both looked back at R.W.. The air was getting a little warm in the kitchen. I quickly sat up, went to the window, opened it, turned on the overhead fan, then sat down again.

I said to Charles, "This is my associate, R.W.. He is also my roommate. R.W., this is my boyfriend, Charles. We thought we would visit with you a little before we went to dinner."

R.W. got up off his chair walked around the table to Charles. R.W. held out his right hand to shake Charles's hand. Charles put out his right hand to shake R.W.'s hand. When they started shaking hands, they began to squeeze each other's hand real tight. Little by little they sidestepped. They continued to sidestep until they went around in a full circle. Charles ended right next to me where he began. They circled each other as if they were two Great Danes sniffing each other's tush. They made complete eye contact. Their eyes penetrated deep into each other's soul, as if animal instinct had just possessed them. My eyes were open wide in anticipation of an incident. I had no idea what had just happened. It was like two dogs sizing up each other. Mmmm, it was interesting, though. R.W. went back to where he was sitting.

When he sat down, he said, "What is your plan tonight? Young lady... make sure you get some good rest. We'll discuss it when Charles is gone." I was about to tell him our plans, but he got up, walked out of the kitchen and out the living room door. We heard his car start up. Then he was gone.

Charles and I looked at each other and shrugged our shoulders. Charles said, "What's his problem?"

"I have no clue." I said. We got in my car to find a place to eat. As we drove away, we decided to go to Perkins.

The hostess sat us in a non-smoking section. I ordered a cheeseburger and fries. Charles ordered eggs and blueberry pancakes.

While we waited for our food, we continued our conversation about R.W.. I asked Charles, "Do you think R.W. has a problem?"

"Oh yes, definitely yes! He was checking me out, like I was his competitor or something. So I just sized him up, too. Just to let him know that I wasn't afraid of him. My question is, why was he sizing me up?"

I said, "Maybe he likes me."

Charles replied, "That could be, or maybe he just wants what's between your legs."

Our food came. I started to lick my fries, seductively. Charles just grinned.

"So," I said, as Charles looked at me with blueberry pancakes halfway to his mouth, "I'm really hungry, can we just eat and go home?"

He swallowed his last bite. He said, "I'm done, what's taking you so long?" Charles left a five-dollar tip. We got up and left the restaurant.

I noticed it was getting dark. The sunset was purple and red across the clouds. It was very romantic. We got in the car. I drove away and headed towards home. I gently placed my right hand on Charles upper thigh. He slowly worked his hand up my skirt. Surprise! I wore no underwear! He liked that, yeeeowza! My breathing increased when he gently slid his fingers inside me. I took a big sigh. I opened my eyes wider so I could concentrate on the road in front of me. I checked my rearview mirror with a quick glance.

The black Porsche was following me again. How the heck did he know I was in America? He had to be connected to the Brotherhood Inc. They were the only ones that knew I had come here. I didn't care at the time. I was in the middle of sexual pleasure! Nothing was about to ruin my night. I hadn't got me some for a year. I had determined to get some sex that night. When we got home my "black wonder"- that's what I sometimes call Charles when I'm really horny, -would strike again!

I remembered in Europe when I was really horny, I e-mailed him this letter:

"The Black Wonder strikes again! The National Weather Bureau has issued a severe thunderstorm building South of the primal nature on the tropical genital regions. The storm will be striking shortly after midnight. All beautiful women are advised to seek shelter in their bedroom. They should be naked and ready for pouncing lessons. The last time the Black Wonder struck was with a Factor of F5. This was the largest we have ever seen on record since the last orgasm. Those women who have not experienced the threat of a Black Wonder should be prepared naked and wet! Sincerely, still horny, Sonthy!"

Charles said he really like that e-mail. Hey, a woman has to do what she's got to do!

Oooh, I was just feeling extraordinary tingles when we pulled into my driveway. We quickly got out of the car, and ran to the front door. I opened it in a wild frenzy, and we made a mad dash for the bedroom. The whole time, we were running and stumbling to the bedroom. We were unbuttoning our clothes, unzipping our pants, and leaving a trail of sexual scent in the air.

Charles flung my bedroom door open. We kissed and groped each other as we fulfilled all imaginable sexual needs. The bed was a little squeaky, but soon I had tuned it out. I buried my moist tongue inside Charles mouth. We kissed and sucked juices from each other's mouths. Ah, oh, it was like tangy kiwi mixed with a little nectarine. I roughly kissed his neck. I licked down his shoulders and over his chest. I sucked his nipples. He softly ran his fingers through my sandy, blonde hair. He was on his knees, but I pushed him onto his back. I ran my tongue down his rippled abdomen. There it was, "my chocolate teaser." I opened my mouth and deeply inserted it. It made sucking and moist sounds as I moved it in and out. With puckering lips, I licked the large arrow shaped soft head. He thrust back his head and moaned with a deep, gusty, "ah." His eyes were closed, but lightly flickered. His long eyelashes looked like butterfly wings as they moved up and down. His stomach tightened. His biceps bulged as surmountable pleasure filled his body. He grabbed two handfuls of bed sheets, and at the same time, he thrust his pelvis forward. I continued to thrust his member in and out of my wet and slippery mouth. He opened his mouth wide and licked his lips. He moaned with exhilarating intensity. I saw tears coming down his cheeks. I felt large amount of salty gush suddenly rush into my throat. I swallowed. I drank some water that I always kept on my night table. I quickly sat on it. It was very thick and hard. I sighed as I felt the large muscle slide inside me. I pushed my hips until my super pubic area meshed with his. I slid my hands under his round butt, then I thrust forward harder than before. Mmmm, that felt so good. Ah, oh,ooh, mmm, yeaaa, oh God, yes. It was going in very deep. I had almost forgotten what it was like. Huh, huh,mmm, nah, huh. I grabbed both his shoulders and thrust as hard as I could. Ooooooh, that hurts good! Wow! I was just beginning. The tip of that hard thing hit something deep inside that made me turn into jelly, my arms and legs began to quiver. I had goosebumps all over my back, arms, and legs. I was slowly losing consciousness. I suddenly had an impulse to go faster. I responded to that urge. I was pushing in and out, so hard and so violent. I was moaning so loud that I didn't realize R.W. in my bedroom, yanking Charles from under me.

Charles, at first, didn't know what was happening. He was butt naked. R.W. put him in a headlock and dragged him down the stairs along with the blankets and sheets. They wrestled around the living room throwing each other around like two bucks whose antlers got stuck together. They knocked over the coffee table, the love seat, and the two lamps. When my mind finally figured out what was going on, suddenly, a rush of violent anger flashed through my body. I quickly put on some clothes and made a mad dash for the living room. I ran into the kitchen, grabbed a large meat knife, quickly leaned over R.W.'s back, who was in the middle of pounding Charles's face into smithereens, and put the knife to his throat.

I loudly yelled, "Move a fucking muscle and you will see God tonight!"

R.W. froze. Then he softly said, "Okay, I'm letting go. See? I let go. Now, I'm going to just sit down right there, okay?"

I said, "Yea, go ahead."

Charles was bleeding all over the place. There was blood on the white carpet, on the white sofas, and on my nice blankets and sheets.

I said to R.W., "What the hell is going on here? No! I don't even fucking want to hear it! You clean up this fucking mess, you asshole! I'm taking Charles to the hospital and when I get back, you better have some damn answers!"

I got a cool, wet wash rag and placed it on Charles right puffy eye. I help him out the door and into my car. I drove to the emergency room.

The emergency room was crowded. Charles didn't say a word on the way down. He was out of it. The doctors saw him. We filled out a police report, and we left the hospital. Charles was feeling much better.

On our ride back home.... I mean to a hotel, he asked me again, "What's his problem? Is there something you're not telling me?"

I paused for a moment before answering him, trying to figure things out. I said, "You know Charles, I haven't a clue. I just met him this week. He said he knew my mother from way back, but I don't know who he is. I really don't know why he acted so jealous. That's all I can figure out. He's just jealous because you have me and he doesn't. I really don't know why he should be jealous though. I've never met him in my life except for this week."

Charles thought for a while, then said, "Well, I think I'll stay here in the hotel for the night. I'll leave for home tomorrow. I have a lot of things to get done."

I said to Charles, "Look, I'm very sorry I brought you into this. I didn't know he was going to respond to you like that."

Charles held out his hands and said, "Hey Sonthy, it's okay. I'm not too badly hurt. Why don't we just snuggle? Can you see me off tomorrow? Just send my bags to me. I'll cover the charge." I nodded yeah, and we cuddled. I fell asleep fully clothed.

The next morning came fast. We cleaned up, then headed for the airport. Charles took the first flight from Minneapolis to Chicago. We had an hour before it would leave. We went to get some coffee and breakfast. When we were eating, I told him how much I missed him. He said he missed me too.

Charles asked, "You make enough money, why can't you get your own house? Why do you have a roommate?"

I replied, "Frankly Charles, I haven't consider buying my own house. It never crossed my mind. I have so many things going on in my life; I just spaced that out. Besides, I consider Mom's house my house."

As soon as I said, "Mom's house," my cordless began to ring. I excused myself and answered it. "The Son."

"Shining Bright," the voice on the other end said.

"Mom! It's you. Boy, have I got news to tell you! Can I call you back in fifteen minutes? Charles has to catch his flight back to Chicago."

Mom paused for a little bit. She said, "Why is he leaving so early? He just got here yesterday. I didn't even get to see him yet."

I said, "Mom, I'll explain it in fifteen minutes. Bye-bye."

"Okay, Dear," she said. I hung up.

Charles looked at me and kept looking. I said, "What was the matter, Charles?"

He lovingly replied, "I miss your mother. I like her a lot. You guys have a good relationship. I wish I knew my mother."

I didn't know what to say so I got up and hugged him, then said, "Lets go catch that airplane." I gave him a kiss.

He turned around and walked through the tunnel to the airplane. He lifted his right hand up to wave goodbye, then he yelled, "I'll e-mail you!" Into the plane he went.

I stood there to watch the plane taxi. It taxied down the runway, then it lifted into the clear, blue sky. I kept an eye on it until it became a tiny black spot in the air. My knees felt weak. Some powerful emotions were bubbling up inside me. I continued to look at the black spot until it faded. Something was happing to me. I felt large teardrops streaming down both my cheeks. I was crying silently. I didn't even know why I was crying. Charles was my best friend. I had never had a best friend. My mom was my best friend. Now Charles was gone. I felt cheated and betrayed. That fucking R.W. Who in the hell did he think he was? Some more tears came out as I walked to my car. I just kept wiping them away. I felt so bad for Charles. My compassion inside was so painful. I was mad, sad, and empathetic at the same time. Hell, I had so many emotions running in me, all I really wanted to do was see my mom.

I got in my Mitsubishi. The minute the door was closed, I pressed that one button on the phone that had mom's phone number in its memory. I put mom on speakerphone. I needed my hands to drive and wipe the tears from my eyes. I sat in the car for a little bit before I pressed the "send" button. I had to get myself under control. It was hard. I had never experienced so many emotions at the same time. I felt like a basketcase. I started driving out of the parking lot. I remembered that it was Saturday. I started thinking what I had to do for Monday. Oh yeah, Mr. Jerk Face, R.W., was supposed to show me my new responsibilities. I thought I would go talk to mom. I would talk to R.W. later, at dinner.

I pressed the "send" button. The phone rang. Mom answered it, "The Savitri's."

"Hi mom. It's me."

Mom paused to listen and then said, "Are you feeling alright, Dear? There's something wrong. Do you want to talk about it?"

I started crying out loud, "Mom. I need to talk to you." I started sniffing.

Mom said, "It'll be alright, Dear. I'm right here. I'll make you some hot chocolate. Hurry now, but be careful driving."

"A- a-alright, I'll be careful."

I stepped on the gas just a little as I entered thirty-five W. The car was up to one-hundred miles per hour and stable. The rush of the car's power got my mind off of my situation for a little while. I picked up the phone and called R.W.. The phone rang. He picked it up.

"R.W.," he said.

I replied, "This is The Son. I'm letting you know that I'll be home tonight. I'm buying dinner. Do you want anything in particular?"

He quietly said, "I'll do the pizza thing, sausage."

I said, "Okay. Sausage pizza it is. I'll be home at six. Bye." Then I hung up.

I pulled into mom's driveway. Mom saw me coming and stood in the open doorway with a mug of hot chocolate in her hand. She gave me a careful hug. I made sure that I didn't spill my hot chocolate on her nice, shiny wooden floors. We went inside and sat at the kitchen table. That's where we always had our serious discussions. I told mom about R.W..

I said, "Can you imagine that!? Smack in the middle of a great orgasm!"

Mom said, "Did you finish coming?"

I said, "No! I still have pent-up energy! I figure I'll go to Chicago next weekend and finish the job."

Then we both said, "The job's not done until the woman's done." Mom and I always used the phrase whenever we were talking about having sex. Then we started to laugh. Ah, I felt much better.

Mom hesitated a little and then she spoke, "Honey, Dear?...." When she said, "Honey, Dear," in the same sentence, I knew it was bad news. She continued, "Honey, Dear, did you notice the men hanging around the house? And the ones hanging around outside?"

I said, "Yea what's that all about?"

She replied, "Those were your father's gift to me to provide protection and security."

I quickly interjected, "Are there any cute ones?"

"Oh, yeah, I've had to use my vibrator a couple of times. Then I went and visited your father and got me some. I got really lonely. But I'll talk to you about that later when we go shopping. I hope you want to go shopping," mom said.

"Oh yeah!" I said with enthusiasm.

Mom continued, "Those men said they noticed a black Porsche with a Masked Man in it since you've came back."

I quickly grabbed Mom's arm, leaned over the kitchen table, looked around from side to side and said in a whisper, "He's been following me, too. He followed me the whole year when I was in Europe. I got used to him. So, I began to ignore him. Did he really start coming shortly after my arrival?"

Mom nodded. I thought, mmm, it's got to be somebody from the Brotherhood, Inc. Mom looked around, too, then leaned over the table and whispered, "My security tried to speak to him, but whenever they would approached the car, he would zoom away."

I said, "I'm so sick of him. One of these days, I'm just going to walk up to his car to talk to him myself.... mom?"

"Now, now don't do that dear." She replied.

I paused for a moment, then spoke, "Have you ever had any guys fight over you, mom?"

Mom quickly answered, "Your dad and John, down the street, fought over me during prom night. John was slow dancing with me when your dad wanted to cut in. That didn't go over well with John, so, he took a swing at your father. Your father ducked his punch, then came back with an upper cut right in the chin. Your dad laid him flat cold on the floor. I told your dad, if he would stop fighting for the rest of his life, I'll date him. So he quit fighting and here we are today."

I replied, "Why did you choose dad?"

Mom thought for a little bit, then said, "Your dad's eyes always got excited whenever he would see me. I liked the undivided attention. Doubt is the key element of pain in all relationships. Faith and trust are also the key element of pleasure. If there is a reason to doubt, then there is evident reason to feel pain. Many emotions are based on faith and trust, or doubt and fear. You have to decide what your relationship is based on."

"Well, Charles is very manly and civilized. He wouldn't fight if his life counted on it. Sometimes he's too civilized, but I trust him. Some men really need their head pounded. R.W. could use a little pounding," I angrily replied.

Mom wanted to go shopping, so I got a chance to drive her new Mercedes. We spent all afternoon shopping. Her security goons followed us wherever we went. They always walked about five yards behind us. At first it was cool, but then it became annoying. At five o'clock, I said my good-byes to mom and went home.

I called ahead to Godfathers Pizza from my car phone. I did the drive through thing and left. I pulled in the driveway, grabbed the pizza, and briskly walked to the door. R.W. saw me coming and opened the doors. Thank God, too, because my hands were hot. R.W. took the pizza from me. He walked over to the kitchen table, sat the pizza down, got us some cola, and sat. He bowed his head, said some kind of mumble jumble grace, then started in on the pizza.

I watched him for a while. Man, he must have been hungry. I was still mad at him. I ate a few slices, then drank my cola. When I was done, I went into the living room. The whole time we were eating, I didn't say a word. I was too upset. I thought it would be a good idea if he did the talking.

When I entered the living room, it was as if nothing had ever happened. The place was spic-n-span. Woosh! This guy was amazing! He always seemed to be under control, except when he beat up Charles. He didn't win any brownie points with me! Hah! I think not!

I sat down on the long sofa in the living room. He came and sat right next to me. I got up, moved to the love seat, then sat down again. He didn't move. I think he got my message. If he didn't, I was just going to make sure he did. I sat, calmly, with my legs and arms crossed, waiting for his explanation.

He finally spoke up. He said, "I'm sorry. I really messed things up. I'm not very good with my feelings. Please forgive me. Can I make it up to you?"

I forcefully said, "Yeah, stay the hell out of my fucking business!" Oh, I was still lit like a fuse. Then I took a deep breath, composed myself, and slowly said, "If you behave so barbaric again, I'm going to move out. Now what was your problem?"

R.W. was taken back a little. He didn't realize that he had a real problem. He actually thought he was being manly. Manly, my ass, that was explicitly foolishness in my book. I let him know it too!

I said, "Fighting is the most foolish thing that men who are still boys do. Real men face their conflicts and learn from them, then make it useful. Do you understand me, or am I just talking to myself? If you want to fight then let's go in the backyard and we can duke it out, just don't get in my business. I have zero tolerance for idiots."

He absorbed it better than I thought he would. He said, "I'm really sorry. Look, the moment I saw you, something inside me went soft. I want you very much. Again, I'm sorry."

I wrinkled up my eyebrows. I was a little surprised and confused. I said, "What did you say?"

He rephrased what he just said. He said, "You are my desire. I want you like a man wants to live. I immediately wanted you the minute I saw you. I know I want you forever."

I said to him in plain English, "I am not for your wanting. I choose who I will be with or not be with. Right now, I choose to be with Charles. Is that clear? You will not interrupt my business, or you'll find me kicking your little behind. If you want to do things with me, just ask me. I am intrigued by you. Besides, you're not that bad looking."

R.W. replied, "Well at least you don't think I'm ugly. Can we do something tomorrow after work? I have a lot to show you."

I paused for a long time. I thought about his polite demeanor, which was so charming. Those big blue eyes and those long eyelashes, I couldn't help but say yes. So, I said, "Maybe. Of course we can! I was just joking."

He sighed a big relief. He gave me a hand, and I shook it. Thank God it was over. I hated going through emotional bullshit! It's just not for me. As handsome as he was, if he would have made a move when I told him not to, I would have slit his throat without a second thought. Good thing he wised up.

R.W. looked away, then quickly met my eyes again. He asked me, "Would you have slit my throat?"

I answered, "Hell yeah, without a thought!"

Then he said, "Well I'm glad you didn't."

I smiled and said, "I'm glad I didn't either. Just don't give me another chance. I might just do it." We both laughed. I was glad it was over.

Monday came quickly. R.W. and I took the day off. He wanted to show me what I was supposed to be doing. We got some ice cream cones, then went for a walk around Lake Harriet. At first, he didn't say a thing. He looked like he was really thinking. Then He said, "The reason the company brought you back here to the States is for you to entertain their customer executives. What I do in the evening is entertain the female executives. You are supposed to entertain the male executives they assign to you."

I replied, "Well that's not so hard. Minneapolis and St. Paul have a lot of things going on."

He looked at me, and rephrased what he just said, "Let me rephrase what I just said, just so we're on the same page. Your contract said you agreed to entertain men by sexual intercourse. Did you read the fine print?"

I said, "No, I didn't read the fine print. They can't make me sleep with any executive. My vagina is mine, no matter what I signed. I'll do with it what I want. I won't prostitute myself. Have you been prostituting yourself the whole time after you entered this business?"

R.W. quickly replied, "They say we are suppose to think of it as public relations, not prostitution. But indeed it is prostitution. Yes, I have. I work in the office in the daytime and at night, I go sleep with some loser bitch they assign me. They only hire the prettiest and most handsome people to sleep with the executives."

I thought that was preposterous. I said. "This is most disgusting!" By now we had already walked a good half a mile around the lake.

He said, "If you refuse to do what they want, you will pay some serious consequences until they terminate you."

"What!? Do you mean they just kill you?" I excitedly said.

R.W. slowly spoke now, "I'm not supposed to tell you this. I'm just telling you because I love you, and I want to marry you. They have the Terminator check out all the new people. He usually wears a black ski mask and drives a black Porsche."

I quickly replied, "I knew that idiot that had been following me in Europe was from this damn company."

R.W. quietly said. "That's the first consequence if you refuse to do what they say."

I said, "Well that's just bullshit."

R.W. continued. "They put fear in you to try to get you obedient."

I wasn't afraid of shit, except for God. I said to R.W., "If they started fucking with me, I'll get real pissy. When I get pissy, the lights go out!"

R.W. jokingly replied, "I've felt the knife of your wrath around my throat. It could kill a person." We both laughed.

The lake was very beautiful and still. There were people all over the place. There was a band playing at the Amphitheater as we walked by. There were hundreds of young kids dancing to the song, *Danger Zone*. The band was wild. For a minute, I started shaking it. R.W. laughed, then he said, "I didn't know that you like to dance. You're pretty good."

"Yea, I love to dance. I go dancing with my mom quite a bit," I eagerly said.

I thought we would stop and dance, but R.W. immediately said, "I'd love to stay and dance, but we have to hurry and clear away from all these people. I have more to tell you about The Brotherhood, Inc." So, we briskly and silently walked one hundred yards past the band.

R.W. suspiciously looked behind us, then quietly whispered, "Did they let you see the warehouses of organs?"

I questioned him and said, "What! The organ warehouses, what's that?"

R.W. leaned over, put his arm around me, then said, "They didn't show you did they?"

I shook my head, "No."

He said, "When I was in Europe, they gave me clearance to enter into all the warehouse that had human organs. What they do is they get DNA samples of each employee, then create clones of you from your DNA. Then they put the cloned person under anesthesia and gut their organs out. Then they preserve the organs in these warehouses. It's kind of like giant wholesale stores, full of human organs. The organs go from there to the black market. They eventually end up in hospitals around the world for organ transplants. So, my dear lady, there is another one of you, probably being grown as we speak. It's probably just starting to walk."

I was taken aback. I didn't know what to say. It took me a few minutes to think about my being cloned, and then gutted for organ transplants. I said, "What else do they do?"

R.W. said, "Well, the reason they have us work together is so we can have a baby together."

I wrinkled my eyebrows down and said, "Have a baby? What the hell! I'm suppose to have a baby with you? For God's sake!"

R.W. quickly looked around, put his hand over my mouth and said, "Ssssssh let me finish. We are supposed to look like a family. What they do is they breed us like animals, and that's how they get their new gene pool. They remove the kid away from you once the child is about a year old. Then, they clone that child, also. They give the child to another couple to raise him or her. Soon, we'll be assigned a child to take care of so we'll look like a family."

I looked at R.W. in disgust. I had to throw up. I ran to a nearby garbage can, put my head in it and puked. R.W. was very kind. He helped me up. Then, he gave me his handkerchief. I took it to wipe my mouth. I looked at R.W. in perplexity and said, "This is the worst thing I've ever heard in my entire life!"

I didn't know what to do. R.W. said, "I'm not finished; there is more. After they gut the organs out of the person, then the person is dead. They use as much of the body they can use, then burn the rest."

Okay, I had heard about enough of this shit! So, I told R.W. not to tell me anymore. I said, "I've had all I can swallow for today, if you don't mind."

R.W. was nice about it. We quit talking about the company. We walked the rest of the way around the lake. R.W. kept his arm around me. I just let him. It was comforting. I put my head on his shoulder as we walked back to the car. I was silent for the rest of the day. Now I knew why R.W. was always calm. You had to be in order to digest all that crap!

We got home. R.W. went to sit on the long sofa. I walked over to him, sat down, then put my head on his lap, before I knew it, it was in the morning. R.W. was still sitting on the sofa, but I had a blanket on me. He's so sweet. He put a blanket on me.

I sat up, tired and groggy. I looked at R.W., then said, "I fell asleep. Did you sleep?"

R.W. replied, "No. I stayed up and watched you snore."

I started to laugh. I said, "What do I sound like?"

He said, "It sounded like a baby pig snorting."

When he said "pig," at first, I laughed. Then, I had a flash back of my dream of the farmer and the pig. I said to him, "We're kind of like pigs on a farm being bred for the slaughter aren't we?"

R.W. nodded "Yes."

I got up and got dressed for work. Into the lab I would go. Let's make more humans to butcher. I was very sarcastic that day. I was in a bad mood. R.W. told me too much. My perception of this company had changed. Everything made sense to me; the way they treated me was too good. My salary was normal, but they put me in a house, shuffled me around in their limo, and gave me their royal treatment. Well, I knew one thing, I was not a prostitute! They had already stolen my DNA, now they wanted to prostitute me? Fuck that!

The week went by pretty fast. Things were normal at work and around the house. R.W. was a perfect gentleman. My heart was starting to get feelings for the guy. I had only known him for two weeks and it felt like I had known him all my life. I thought I had started to fall in love. I still thought falling in love was for the birds. I would just ignore it. When he mentioned that bullshit earlier about wanting to marry me, well... I just ignored that, too.

Friday was here. I had had enough of playing house. I called up Charles to ask him if I could visit him. He said it was okay. I flew to Chicago right away after work. I had my bags packed before I went to work. The minute I got off work, and got home, I called a cab to take me to the Minneapolis/St. Paul International Airport.

I arrived in Chicago on schedule. Charles was right there to pick me up. We rented a room in the Hyatt Regency. We ordered some dinner. It was evening. I didn't really feel like doing anything spectacular that night. So, Charles agreed to stay inside. We ate, then I got ready for bed. It was only eight o'clock. Charles and I watched some romantic movie and snuggled. I was still tired. I fell asleep. I woke up about seven o'clock the next morning.

Charles had eggs and toast ready for breakfast. Charles and I sat down to eat. I knew that Charles didn't like me working for The Brotherhood, Inc.. He never said anything, but I could tell in his attitude. Whenever I talked about work, he went silent.

I sat down to eat. Charles sat next to me at the table. I looked at him for a while. I didn't say a thing. Finally, I spoke up. I said, "Charles why don't you like the company I work for?"

Charles said, "Dad didn't like it, and I don't like it."

"But why don't you like it?" I asked. He went silent again. He quickly ate his food, got up, and went over to the bed. He laid down staring at the ceiling. I said, "Hey buddy, what's the matter? Are you getting an attitude on me? Do you want me to return to the Cities?"

I slowly got up, walked over to the bed, and took his hand. He looked like he was about to cry. I gently caressed his hand with my right palm. Then, he started to cry silently. I had no clue what I just said. How did I make him cry? I thought to God, hey God! What's his problem? What did I say wrong? Men are so confusing sometimes. He acted like a child. I got a little uncomfortable.

I got up, paced back and forth in front of the window, and ran my fingers through my hair. I pushed it back out of my eyes. I paced a little more, then I stopped and looked at him. He was just staring at me, watching me pace. I hated emotional garbage. If I could have lived without my emotions, I would have. I wasn't the best person to deal with people's emotions. Whenever I got too much emotion in me, I just got sick, unless I was angry with someone. Then, it was time to kick some ass!

Charles finally said, "Sonthy come and sit down right here." Then, with his left hand he patted the edge of the bed next to him. I cautiously walked over to the bed. I sat down, facing him. I took his hand again and started caressing it. He said, "That Brotherhood Corporation you work for is nothing but doo-doo."

Charles never swore. He used soft words, like doo-doo, or he'd even make up a few, if he was really mad. One time, he was mad at me for something really dumb. It was that night in Europe he was trying to pick up that big-breasted bimbo. He called me "bufunkle." I didn't know what it was so I just ignored it. Now, he says the company I work for is doo-doo? I asked him why he thought that.

He replied, "That company had my mother shot. She used to work for them as a lab specialist. She wouldn't screw some executive guy, she told them she was married. They didn't like it, so they shot her. I hate that company! But since you work for them, I thought I would keep my opinions to myself."

I asked, "Did the police arrest the man that did it?"

He said, "They don't know who did it. The last description they had of the murdered was a guy dressed in black with a mask, driving a black Porsche."

I quickly grabbed Charles' hand. I told him that when he came to visit me in Europe, a black Porsche had followed us the whole time."

He said to me, "You're going to be assigned some executive to screw to keep happy, you know? Are you going to do it?"

I looked at him and shook my head side to side. Then said, "I had a hard enough time sleeping with you. Hell, I'll admit to God, and the whole world that I was always horny, but I'm no prostitute! You should know me better than that. I would kill anyone who tries to make me go against my will."

Charles looked at me and smiled. He sat up, placed both his hands on my arms, and pulled me to him. There I was, lying on top of him. My little tinker bell, the magic spot was ringing. I felt his bulge in his pants rubbing on my super pubic area. I buried my lips into his. We kissed passionately. I drank his moist champagne like water in a desert. His hands wildly fondled my breasts. He rashly unbuttoned my blouse. His whole face fell into my bosom. He kissed my pomegranates. He sucked on my juicy melons. His lips puckered, like sweet and sour wine was being poured into his cheeks from my succulent breasts. My springs were flowing now! He slowly reached into my panties. Then he placed his long, hard, thick and delicious golden treasure inside me. I couldn't wait for it. He must have known why I came to see him. My fountain of youth was rushing into the night, glittering with moon's light, as we dove into it to play with the porpoises. Nature was working with us. Mmmm, oooh! Yes, huh, huh, ooh, mmm. Push, stop, over okay, push harder. Ooh, mmm, huh, oh yeah! Oh yeah! Oooooh. I saw a comet go by. I was fast asleep. I woke up for a pee break. It was five o'clock. I went to the bathroom. When I was finished, I came back to bed to snuggle next to Charles, then fell asleep, again.

It was Sunday. Charles and I stayed inside all day to have sex. We did it on the kitchen table, on the floor, in the shower. We did it standing up, on the bed facing each other, and my favorite position was the doggy position. We did it that way, too! I felt better afterwards. All that pent-up energy was well distributed. The best way to be at peace with life was just to have multiple orgasms.

Mom and I used to say, "The reason I do everything I do, is to have sex!" We'd always got a kick out of saying that because many times it seems like it.

Charles was happy I came. He escorted me to the airport. I caught my flight home. It was ten o'clock when I got to the house. I came in through the garage door, hoping R.W. wasn't home. I wasn't in the mood for anything serious. I was in a quiet, somber mood. I went upstairs to bed. R.W. wasn't even home. He left a note that said he had to go entertaining. He would be back in the morning. That was good. I fell asleep.

Chapter 5

The Rise to Power

It had been a year since I have been back to the States. I saw the black Porsche follow me a couple of times when I first got back, but I just ignored him. I am getting good at ignoring him. The man in the Black Mask had not shown his face for months. He decided to quit bothering me. I am glad and relieved. I did not need anymore anxieties.

Nobody had asked me to sleep with anybody, so far. I had been doing really well at work. My immediate supervisor really liked me. I had just gotten a raise, twenty thousand dollars extra per year! It took me two years to finally get a raise. My boss said that I was sharp and alert. She said that not much got past me. I was taught to listen to what people didn't say, as well as what they did. Mom always said, "People say many things, but it's the result of their actions that says it all." I believe that, too.

The other weekend, Charles came to visit. He was the sweetest, most faithful guy I had ever met. He was kind and considerate. I wish I had great passion for him. He would make the best husband. He was very consistent and dependable.

Again when Charles came over (he had been over a dozen times since he and R.W. fought) he and R.W. almost got into another brawl. I made sure that their schedules stayed clear of each other. When they did see each other, it's seemed like a miniature war was about to break out. They just danced circles around each other.

One day, they started to bump chests like students in high school. It looked kind of silly at first, until R.W. took a swing at Charles and missed. Then Charles kicked R.W. in the jewels. That retired R.W. for a while. R.W. had found a new respect for Charles. They eyed each other, periodically, from a distance.

Charles got a little jealous of the time I spend with R.W., but he handled it like a man. I was very proud of him. He knew I was proud of him, too.

R.W. still wanted to marry me. I just didn't get where he got the notion that I was going to marry him. He was very handsome, though. If I wasn't with Charles, I would have considered R.W., already. I didn't even entertain the thought because I was madly attracted to R.W.. I made sure I kept my distance.

R.W. and I did a lot of fun things together. We went to Disney Land for the weekend one time. Again, Charles took it like a man. He knew that I was my own person. I always did what I wanted. Charles knew how to give me plenty of space.

R.W., on the other hand, was always seeking how to get into my space. R.W.'s personality was very strong. He thought that one day I was going to melt into his arms. I thought he was full of shit! The only arms I was going to melt into were my own. R.W. told me a lot about the Brotherhood, Inc. and I had learned a lot about them on my own. R.W. and I went snooping around their warehouses one weekend. It's been a thing of ours ever since he told me all that junk during our first walk around Lake Harriet.

One time we rented a Lear Jet, took three days off work so we could have a long weekend, and flew over to Europe to go snooping. It was fun! We bought some navy blue outfits. We put some pantyhose over our heads. We got up at one in the morning and drove to the warehouse. We got past security very easily. They were a bunch of young horn-dogs, so I lured them by taking off my shirt. They liked my bare breasts. I blew a few kisses at them, then took down my pants to my knees. I was standing there in my panties. Then they came down out of their booths to me. R.W. was hiding around the corner. He hammered them with a good right fist. They were both out. We drugged them up so they would be gone for the night. We took their jeep and all their keys and went to the warehouses.

We pulled up to the first warehouse. The sign said, "Limbs and Outer Extremities." We went through the doors, quietly. There were people working all over the place. We quietly tiptoed around the back hallways, being sure to avoid the cameras. We sprayed a coupled of cameras with black paint at the place where we were going to take our samples. It was amazing what I saw. They had rows of living people, laying on operating tables, plump full of anesthetics. They were numbered on their foreheads, and on their left hands were bar codes. There were no names for any of them. I saw doctors and nurses taking limbs and parts off the bodies. They worked methodically. There were other doctors who would receive those limbs and then grew them to maturity. This stuff was spectacular.

We left that building, and drove to another warehouse called "Embryos." We sprayed a few cameras again in the areas where we were going to do our thing. We took samples and pictures. We took all kinds of pictures!

Security got onto us. We made a mad dash for the door. We jumped on the jeep and drove out of the compound! That was very close. Another jeep followed us out the gates, shooting sprays of bullets into the night at our jeep. My heart was pounding. When they started shooting, they scared the living shit out of me. I had never shot a gun in my life. I was driving like a mad woman because I was so scared. R.W. told me to take a few breaths. He pulled out a silver gun with a silencer and shot out the two front tires of the jeep following us. He was a great shot! Wow! I was impressed. We didn't stop. I was topping about eighty all the way to the airport.

We called to our pilot and he was ready for us. We hurried into the plane and the pilot made it into the air with no problem. He didn't say a word to us. He just did his thing. When we got to the Minneapolis/St. Paul International Airport, my blood pressure calmed down a little. R.W. and I hugged each other and grinned. We got into my Mitsubishi and drove home.

When we got in the house, we dumped all our specimens in the downstairs freezer and refrigerator. We had lots of samples from our excursion. That was the only time we came close to getting caught. Usually, they never knew that we were there.

We talked a little about our night and our next plan. I went to give R.W. a hug. He gave me this great big bear hug. I got used to his hugs. R.W. would give me these muscle hugs whenever he was very happy. Then he surprised me. He slipped me a long wet kiss. I grabbed his head and buried my tongue down his throat. I sucked his juices. Charles popped into my mind. I abruptly pushed R.W. away from me, then I walked up to him and slapped him on his left cheek. I didn't say a word. He stared at me with perplexity. I looked him in the eye like I was mad at him, but I wasn't. I had never felt so exhilarated in my life! I pivoted around on my heels, walked up the stairs, and slammed my bedroom door.

The next day, I ignored R.W.. I gave him the silent treatment for a whole week. Man! I wanted him really bad! What was going on here? That whole week my emotions were going haywire. How could that happen just from one kiss? Woo, that was hot! It was smoking! I kept it from Charles. I was so confused! I didn't know what the hell was happening. Whenever I would see R.W., my knees got weak. My head got real fuzzy. I couldn't think. I figured that the best thing for me to do was to stay away from him. At least until my head cleared.

When I went to work in the morning, I picked up the "In House Newsletter." There was a whole page on our excursion. The Brotherhood was suspicious. They beefed up their security around the office. In fact, they beefed up security in the entire corporation.

There was a lot of talk through the whole company about our last excursion. Some people liked our event. They thought we were modern day Robin Hoods! Others thought that they should find out who was doing it and fire them if it was somebody within the company. Others thought it was an outsider trying to blackmail the corporation. Most of the people really didn't care one way or another. It was simply just something to talk about. There was a little article from the two twins. The article talked about the twins' opinion on the matter. The article basically said they weren't too concerned, but the conspirators will be found.

I wasn't too concerned about getting caught. I thought most of the security people weren't too bright anyway. The day in the lab was just another day in research. There was nothing new besides the newsletter. I got off work a little early.

My boss informed me that I was to have a meeting with a Dr. Studdleman, a prominent surgeon. So, she let me off early. That was the first I had heard about this meeting. What was the meeting supposed to be about anyway? I didn't know.

I drove home and took of my shoes as I came into the house. I sat down in the living room just to unwind. Shortly after I came in, R.W. came. He did his stuff and went downstairs. He didn't say a word to me. I wondered if he was mad at me? I sat by myself on the sofa for about a half-hour. I got up, walked over to the kitchen, and pressed the button to the intercom system. I sternly spoke into it and said, "R.W. may I have a word with you?"

R.W. replied, "I'll be up in a minute." He came up about five minutes later. He sat on the sofa opposite me. There was some silence for a couple of minutes. I took full advantage of the silence. I observed his beauty. Then he said, "Did you want to talk to me about something?"

I stumbled for words. I was starting to feel a little fuzzy around him. I timidly asked, "Who is Dr. Studdleman?"

He answered, "Dr. Studdleman is a surgeon from the hospital downtown. He is the chief of hospital operations. Why?"

"Well my boss said I was supposed to have a meeting with him this evening,"

R.W. said, "Dr. Studdleman is a very important man. He is one of our best customers. He must bring about thirty million dollars to the Brotherhood, Inc. He is also Head Surgeon of the National Surgeons Association."

I looked at R.W., and felt awful for treating him badly the last couple of weeks.

"Hey," I said.

"Hey what?" he returned.

"I'm sorry for slapping you."

"That's okay. Sonthy, I deserved it," he said.

I looked at him very cautiously, then said, "I didn't tell you my name was Sonthy. How did you know my name?"

R.W. had that handsome grin again. He said, "Sonthy Savitri, Sonthy, Sonthy Savitri. Hey, Sonthy Savitri! Are you doing laundry?"

I gasped for air. I put both my hands over my mouth and just sat there staring at him. Then he said, "You shouldn't have put me in the dryer. But I still love you."

I stood up and ran to him. I threw myself on him and started to cry. I was sobbing uncontrollably. He held me tight.

I said, "Where have you been all these years. I had been hurting so badly when your parents moved away." I started crying some more. I couldn't help it. It was like a giant flood inside of me. A dam seemed to have burst deep inside me when he spoke. I didn't know what to say or do. I was weak all over. I just collapsed in his arms. I cried for about fifteen minutes.

When I was done. I stood up and slapped him on the right cheek. I said, "Why didn't you tell me it was you a year ago, Reggie Wheaties? I've been living with my childhood friend all this time, and you kept it from me! You're a schmuck!"

He grabbed my hands and pulled me down to the sofa. He got up, then motioned for me to sit down. He said, "Wait here a minute. I have something for you downstairs."

He ran downstairs like a child. His eyes were beaming with excitement. A couple of minutes passed. I was still sitting where he left me. He came stumbling up the stairs with a little black box in his right hand. He took my left hand and slid a huge diamond on my ring finger. He got on one knee and said, "Will you marry me. O' Sonthy Savitry. Sonthy, Sonthy, Sonthy Savitry?" He said it just like he used to say it when we were little.

I immediately replied, "Yes, yes, yes, undoubtedly yes!"

He kissed me! Wow! It was like Heaven opened and millions of angels stood around us, singing and blowing their trumpets! I felt so light. Wow! I had never ever felt like this in my life! What a kiss! This was a kiss beyond the universe. I pushed him away. Then I said, "Hey, Reggie, I have to call Mom. Got to tell her the good news!" I was so excited!

I walked over to the kitchen phone and dialed it. The phone rang. Mom picked it up and said, "The Savitri's."

"Hi, Mom! Hey, I have to tell you something. Do you want to come over?"

"Okay, Dear, I'll be there in fifteen minutes. I got to pull the banana muffins out of the oven." Mom was always baking or making something. She gave most of it away to the neighborhood families.

"Bye, Mom," I said.

She replied, "Bye, Dear." I hung up the phone, and e-mailed Dad to call me.

R.W. was sitting at the bar in the kitchen. I was standing between his legs leaning against him. He had this handsome grin. I started talking about the wedding. "It's got to be in a big church," I said.

Reggie said, "Of course, and the wedding festivities have to be as grand as possible!" That was the first time I had ever seen him really excited. He got excited; he was just calm about everything. This time I actually saw enthusiasm. I was very happy. Reggie and I were deep into the wedding talk when the doorbell rang.

I opened the door. "Mom! Come in! Come in!" Reggie got up from the kitchen and walked into the edge of the dining room, leaned around one of the walls to take a peek at us and calmly walked over to the sofa and sat down. I grabbed both of Mom's hands and pulled her to the sitting area. I motioned for her to sit down. We were facing each other. Our knees were touching, as they commonly did when we had something important to say. I raised my left hand with my engagement ring, right at eye level. Her eyes zoomed right on the incredibly radiant diamond!

"Oh!" She yelled. She put her right hand to her mouth. She yelled, "Charles where are you, you handsome Devil!? Let me give you a hug!"

I quickly thought, Oh, Man. Charles. What am I going to do about Charles? His feelings are going to be hurt. I'll have to talk to him in person.

Then I looked at Mom. I said, "Mom." Mom had already got up and started looking for him. She was very excited. Reggie didn't say a thing. I walked over and sat next to Reggie. Then I held his hand. I said again, "Mom! Come sit down."

She came and sat down again. She looked over at me sitting next to Reggie. It had been a year and she still didn't know who he was. She gave me a funny look. She wrinkled her eyebrows into a questioning look.

I said, "Mom, this is my fiancé. Do you remember R.W.?"

She looked at me, then looked at him, then looked at our intertwined hands. After a long time, she finally asked, "How did this happen? I thought you were dating Charles?"

I said, "Mom, I was dating Charles, but we are really good friends. I've gotten to know R.W. very well in the past year. And no, Mom, R.W. and I didn't have sex yet. I decided I love R.W.. I didn't love Charles. Mom, Charles and I were sex partners. That doesn't have anything to do with love. I love R.W.."

Mom looked at me and said, "Sonthy, you always made your own decisions. I hope this one is as wise as most of your others have been." I could tell she was disappointed. She and Dad liked Charles. They had known him for two years now. He was like part of the family.

Mom got up and headed for the front door. I quickly got up, ran behind her and put her in a big long hug. I whispered in her ear, "Mom, it's Reggie Wheaties. You know the kid I threw in the dryer and closed the door? Cute Punk."

Mom slowly turned around with her hands to her mouth in surprise. She briskly walked over to him to inspect him, like some piece of product off a shelf. She gently squeezed his fat cheeks, as if he was still eleven. Then she asked, "How are your folks Reggie?"

Reggie stood up and gave her a hug, then said, "They are just fine, Mrs. Savitry. I just want to know if you're going to send Sonthy to feed me soup if I get sick. That dryer bit took me fifteen years to get over." We all laughed. Mom was happy again. She was proud of me again.

The phone rang while Mom and Reggie were talking. I went to pick it up. "The Son."

"Hi, Sonthy. It's Charles, can we meet somewhere? I have to talk to you." Charles' voice had concern in it. That made me nervous. I hoped he was okay.

I replied, "Are you okay?"

He said, "Yes I'm fine, but it's really important."

I said, "okay, let's meet halfway. How about the Mauston Park Oasis in Mauston Wisconsin off I 90/94, exit 69, Saturday morning at ten o'clock in the morning."

He said, "That sounds great, bye!"

He was exited about something, so that was good. He had me worried for a minute. I said goodbye and hung up.

I told mom that I had to meet Charles in Mauston on Saturday. She sighed and breathed easier. I knew what she was thinking. She thought it would be good if I cleared things up with Charles in person. But I was thinking that myself, anyway. I walked over to her and gave her a kiss on her cheek.

She patted me on the back and said, "Thank you dear. It's getting late. I have to get going. I'll leave you two lovebirds alone. Goodnight."

Mom got up and walked out the door. Reggie and I walked her to her car to see her off. Reggie took one look at the car and said, "Whooa! Nice wheels! Is she rolling in the dough or what?"

I said, "What. She's just rolling in what."

Reggie looked at me and said, "You think you're funny, don't you? I'll show you funny."

He picked me up and carried me inside. He laid me on the floor and started to tickle me. Oh, I was going to get him back. I hated being tickled. I remembered how he used to do that when we were little. I hated it then, and I hated it that day. He knew that, too. We were in the middle of wrestling around on the floor when the doorbell rang.

I got up and opened the door. It was the Zum Man and some middle-aged, partially balding male. He was very well dressed. Reggie got up and sat on the sofa. Reggie knew who the stranger was, but I didn't.

The Zum Man walked over to me, did his little circular walk around me, as if he was inspecting me, and said, "This is Mr. Studdleman. He'll be your date tonight. Wine and dine him and don't forget to entertain him. Give him whatever he wants. Goodnight."

The Zum Man motioned to R.W. and they both walked out the door together. I walked over to the window, there I saw the Zum Man drive away in a limousine. R.W. just got into his own car and drove away.

Mr. Studdleman was walking around, looking at things in the house. He picked up the phone and ordered some Chinese food. Mr. Zum Man must have told him I liked Chinese. I walked over to him and said, "My boss told me that I was supposed to have a meeting with you, but she didn't say what about. So what did you need to see me for?"

Mr. Studdleman said, "I'll talk to you when the food gets here." I had a funny look on my face. It was one of those questioning looks. I was thinking this old man thought he was going to get sex out of me, he had another thing coming. But, he was polite enough, so I just went with the flow.

The food came. I took it and sat down at the table. I served him some of his portion. When he sat down to eat, I said, "Look at my diamond. I got engaged."

He looked and said, "That's lovely. I wish you the best."

He continued eating. I ate all my food, then placed the dishes in the sink. When I was done, I walked back to the dinning room to see what Mr. Studdleman was up to. He was on his way upstairs. I quickly ran behind him with frustration.

I said, "Hey! Hey! Where are you going?"

He ignored me and continued to go up the stairs. He walked down the hall to my bedroom door. He opened it, went inside and started to loosen his tie. He unbuttoned his shirt until his white T-shirt was showing. He took off his pants. What the hell! I thought. Pink boxing shorts with flowers! Who was this guy kidding?

He pointed at me and patted the bed. I walked over to him, and said, "Look sir, I'm not a prostitute. I don't intend to be one. My fiancé has never been with me yet. You're not my type. Besides, I'm not interested."

He reminded me of what the Zum Man said, "Give him anything he wants." I was not about to give him shit!

I told him, "Look Mr. Studdleman, you are a nice man, but I don't think I'm the way to go. Just put your clothes back on and let's just forget about it."

He pulled out a revolver and pointed it at me. Then he said, "I think it's in your best interest to do what I say."

I swallowed a big lump in my throat. I took a deep breath. I slowly and sexually walked to him. I took off my blouse and my pants. I was standing there in my purple underwear. I laid on the bed, then said, "Are you going to continue to point that thing or are you going to do the nasty?"

As I was saying that, I let my breast burst out of my bra. He put the gun down, straddled my thighs and started fumbling with my soft and firm breast. I let him get into it. Then he started reaching down for my vagina. That was when I kneed him in the groin. I gave him a right hook and slammed him against my left fist. His eyes rolled back into his head until the whites of his eyes showed. He was out. I drug him off my bed and onto the floor. I took his gun, with the bed sheets, and shot out one kneecap. Blood splattered in my face. Then I called the police. It was five minutes before they came. I quickly got dressed and answered the door. I escorted them upstairs and told them how he pulled his gun on me and tried to rape me. They called an ambulance and took him away. I went to the police station and filed a report, then they let me go.

I came home to a bloody place. I spent the rest of the night doing laundry. I was so angry! Doing laundry was a good outlet. I was just coming down the stairs with a load of stuff when Reggie walked through the front door. He said, "Let me help you with that, just don't put me in the washing machine."

I said, "Look I'm not in the mood for joking." While he carried the laundry, I silently walked with him to the laundry room. When we got there, I violently shoved the bloody sheets into the washer, put tons of bleach on them along with some laundry soap and then shut the lid. I turned around and leaned against the washer with my butt.

I sighed and thought over the implications of my actions. I knew I was going to have some trouble. I just wished I knew what it would be. Reggie sensed my frustration and started to hug me. I slammed both the palm of my hands on his chest and sharply shoved him back.

He took a few steps back and just stood there looking at me. He didn't say a thing. He walked a couple of steps towards me, gently took my hands, then looked straight into my blue eyes, and said, "I will support you one hundred and thirty percent on any decision you make." He knew very well what I did. He knew that I wasn't going to sleep with that man, but he didn't know to what extent the event escalated.

The minute I saw Reggie's deep blue eyes, I melted. I felt a peace inside me. I slowly walked over to him, put my arms around him, and hugged him. Then I started to cry. Reggie softly said, "We'll get through this together. I'm here."

After my sob time, I explained to him what just transpired. First he said, "Uh, oh."

I said, "What?"

He said, "It's a good thing you are doing laundry. You might as well think of hiding, because The Brotherhood won't tolerate you. They will send their hitman. The man who drives a black Porsche."

Immediately I said, "I knew it! I knew it! I knew that man in the black Porsche was from this damn company! What the hell did I get myself into, Reggie?"

Reggie said, "That's exactly right! Hell is the correct term. That's what you got yourself into. I've been trying to get out for years. I don't think there is a way. They shoot anybody that trys to quit. But if you think of a way, please let me know."

I softly put both my palms on his cheeks. I confidently said, "Everything will turn out alright. Right now I have to go see Charles tomorrow and tell him about our engagement. We are going to meet in Mauston."

Reggie hesitantly replied, "Would you like me to come?"

"I rather tell him myself."

We walked upstairs and made the bed together. I told him that I didn't want to sleep in this bed for a while so I asked him if I could sleep in his downstairs.

That night, I slept with Reggie for the first time. He was a gracious gentleman. He didn't try anything. The minute I laid down, I was out! I slept very soundly that night.

I had a strange dream of angels all around me. In the dream, I got up and went to work. There were angels in the car, in the back seat, on the hood, on top of the car, and jogging along the side of the car. When I got out of the car to go into the lab, there were angels walking beside me. When I finally got to work, there were angels all around the lab. There were angels working beside me. When I went home, there were angels in the house, angels in my garage, angels in the kitchen. There were even angels in the bathroom.

When I woke up I felt really happy and safe. I told Reggie that we had angels all around us. He said, "It's just a dream, Sonthy." We left it at that because we didn't want to fight. Reggie was very sensitive.

When I got in my car to leave for Mauston, Reggie said, "Remember your dream this morning, bye!" Then he kissed me and off I went to Mauston.

My drive to Mauston went great. I drove eighty miles per hour the whole way. Thank God there were no cops. I set my cruise control and cranked up the tunes. I was lost in the land of oblivion. I had no time to do any serious thinking; it was music and velocity!

My mother said if you were going to do anything meaningful, do it with all your heart. Think carefully and comprehensively about what you're going to do before you do it. Weigh your cost, but when you're ready to do it, do it with all your heart. Do it two hundred percent! No thinking, just primal instinct! Mom would say, "Forget your fears, your inhibitions, your attitudes; you've already thought it through, talked it out, cried it down and pondered it inside out, now it's no thinking, just primal instinct!" When I was a kid, even when mom wasn't with me, I would hear her voice inside me, saying, "Think, say and do. But make sure you do!"

When I was in high school, I used to go around chanting. "Think, say, do! There's no thinking, just primal instinct!" Once I decided to do something it was full steam ahead until my mission was accomplished. The only thing that was in a race was me and my schedule.

Mauston was a cute little town. It was very peaceful and friendly. Charles was on time. Actually, I was a little late. We met at the Oasis. The hotel room we rented was small, but it would do.

Charles was excited to see me. But he said he had some good news and bad news. I had some good news and bad news of my own. We walked in the hotel room and sat down at the table. I got up and opened all the curtains to let some sunshine in. It was an exceptionally happy day for me. That dream really effected my emotions.

We sat down to talk. I said, "Charles I want to get to the point."

He quickly interrupted me and said, "Wait! Me first. Look at this girl's picture. Tell me what you think of her."

I took the picture out of his hand. I looked at it. It just looked like a normal picture. I shrugged my shoulders after I looked at her. I handed it back. Charles pushed it back to me again. He said, "Look at it a little longer, because that's my future."

I said, "What do you mean, your future?"

He nervously replied, "Well, I was a little embarrassed when R.W. pulled me off you in the middle of sex. That made me think of my future. I wanted a woman to love and live with forever. I'm talking about marriage. I proposed to Vanessa Trapson and she accepted. I'm engaged, Sonthy."

I squinted my eyes at him, trying to figure out if he was putting me on. Then I said, "Are you putting me on? You're serious about this?"

He nodded.

I said, "Since when?"

He said, "I've known her all my life. Her folks still live by my folks. She's my best friend. She goes to college with me."

In surprise, I sighed a big sigh of relief for both of us. I said, "Wow!"

Charles got up and started pacing back and forth without a word. I said, "Are you alright?"

He quickly sat down, then got back up, paced a little bit, grabbed the top of the chair, turned it around, and finally sat down again. He sat on it like he was riding a horse. The back of the chair was facing me. He was resting his arms on it. I slightly raised my voice and said, "Hey! What's your problem? You said you were all right. Why are you pacing back and forth like an impatient Cheetah?"

He quickly interrupted, "Vanessa and I just had our first sexual intercourse..." He paused; I didn't say anything. I opened my eyes a little wider, because I was surprised about him getting married, but who gives a shit about him having sex with her?

There was a long pause. I finally said, "Charles, I don't give a hoot if you had sex with the girl you want to marry. Congratulations!"

I got up and gave him a big hug. After the hug, I shook his hand. He quickly looked down at my ring. He didn't miss a thing. For a minute there, the way he was acting, I thought it would take all night for me to get to tell him what I had to tell him. He said, "Hey what's that!?"

I said, "Hello Charles, haven't you seen an engagement ring before?"

He was taken aback a little, "Well ah, ...mmm, hh, you're engaged?"

I said very slowly, "Yeah, I am."

"To whom, may I ask? It's not who I think it is, Mr. Shit head! Is it?"

I nodded my head yes.

He angrily said, "Why would you want to marry R.W.? What does he got that I don't got?"

I stood up quickly, and said, "Hey, hey! Easy, now. Don't start comparing yourself with him."

Then he said, "But...?"

I stopped him. I put my index finger over his lips and said, "Shhhh, please sit down."

He slowly turned the chair around and sat down. He was really mad, but he always conducted himself like a man. He was patiently waiting for my explanation. I didn't really feel that I should have to explain myself. I just did what I did. If anybody liked it or didn't like it, who gave a damn? But, Charles was another story. I really cared a lot what he thought. It wasn't because we had been having sex, but because he had been through a lot with me. I thought that I should have explained in person.

So, I said, "Charles, first of all, I didn't even have sex with him yet, not until we're married. Secondly, I don't think it's any of your business. Thirdly, you know that I love you. I don't want you hurt. Can I get another hug, then I'll explain myself."

Charles hugged me again. This time, he held on a little while. Finally, he let go. He had some tears in his eyes. I slowly wiped his cheeks.

He had a reason to be mad. I've never met Vanessa, and Vanessa didn't do anything to me, but R.W. was awful to Charles. When I got back, I planed to put an end to that bullshit!

Charles sat down. I said, "Charles, R.W.'s name was really Reggie Wheat. He kept his identity from me. The whole time since we've been living together, about a year now, I've had this strange pull. My heart has been full of crazy emotions for him. At first, I couldn't explain what was going on. I didn't speak to him for several weeks one time. He took the liberty to kiss me when he wasn't invited. I slapped him and quit talking to him. Reggie was my first love, every since I was a kid. I cried for a couple of years when his parents moved away. It ate at me ever since he's been gone. I'm just a very disciplined person. I don't let my soft side show. You know how I am, Charles."

"When you came into the picture, I decided to move on with my life. I couldn't stay single forever waiting and hoping some lost childhood love would come knocking at my door. I was so mad at God for taking my Reggie from me. Charles, remember when your mother was murdered, that pain you felt? Well, that's how I've been feeling all these years."

Charles nodded. He started crying again. Then, I started crying. We cried for a while, cuddled on the bed the rest of the evening. We finally got hungry and grabbed something to eat.

At dinner, I reached out and told him how much he meant to me. He was the first male that I had ever gotten close to. I told him I wanted him in my life in many other forms for the rest of my life. Just because we weren't having sex, even though it was good, whooo, yeah! Well, I still loved Charles in a different part of my heart. We held hands the whole time we ate.

When we left the restaurant, we had our arms around each other. We grabbed a movie and went back to the hotel. We watched the video, then took off our clothes and cuddled in our underwear the rest of the night. That was very hard for me to do, since his penis was hard and pushing up against my butt. That was the last time we ever snuggled. I finally got to sleep around two o'clock in the morning. I was a little tired when I woke up.

Charles woke up in a really cheerful mood. He was singing. He said, "Sonthy?"

I replied, "Yea." I turned and faced him. I was still getting dressed.

He continued, "Sonthy, I'm sorry for getting angry. I thought I wouldn't ever see you again. I feel that a giant weight has been lifted off of me. I'm very happy for you. Just tell Mr. Reggie Wheat that he has a very special woman. I love you, Sonthy."

I hugged him, and when I pulled away, some tears welled up in my eyes. Charles grabbed me and held me a little. I let him.

This was so awful. I felt that I was losing my best friend, even though I was not. I sighed a deep sigh. Charles wiped my eyes with the tissue from the table. I felt so strange. I felt really good about my decision to marry Reggie, and I didn't feel bad for cuddling with Charles all night.

We were walking to our cars to depart and go our separate ways, when suddenly, I heard some footsteps walking behind me. I quickly turned and got into my Chung Moo Quan stance. I was ready to fight. There was nothing behind me. I turned to Charles and said, "Did you hear that?"

He said, "Shhh, I hear a bunch of foot steps walking around your car."

We both stood real still. We looked around. It was in the middle of the day. Cars were going left and right. People were going about their business, yet I felt a presence besides us.

Our cars were parked side by side, facing opposite each other. Mine was facing south and Charles was facing north, with the driver's side next to each other. We slowly walked over to our cars. We approached, cautiously. Somebody was there. I stopped Charles with my right hand. I motioned for him to quietly circle around the cars, while I bent down and looked underneath. Charles tiptoed around the two cars. I looked underneath. I saw nothing. Charles came back to where I was standing. We slowly continued to walk towards our cars. Suddenly we couldn't get any closer to the cars. We were three feet away. There seemed to be an invisible wall that we couldn't penetrate through. Then both cars violently exploded. The flames shot straight up. The invisible wall contained the explosion. Charles and I fell backwards. We got up and looked around. All the people were standing and staring at our cars torched in large flames.

I opened up my purse and got out my cellular phone. I dialed 911. In less than five minutes the police were there and the ambulance was right behind, along with the fire department. The fire department tried to spray the cars, but the invisible wall was still there. They sprayed and sprayed, but nothing happened.

Suddenly, Charles' car exploded again with a big bang. The whole crowd shouted and screamed. The flames finally died down a little. We stood there for forty-five minutes, waiting for something else to happen. All of a sudden, my eyes were open, as if I had dark glasses on and took them off. I looked at the burning cars and there were angels surrounding the two cars in a giant circular barricade.

These angels were very large. They were about thirteen feet tall. One of them must have weighed about as much as my car. They had broad shoulders with gold wings spread out behind them. Each wing was touching another angel's wing tip, which was also spread out. The angels were facing the crowd. They had large swords in their hands, about seven feet long. They were the largest swords I had ever seen in my life! I recognized one of the angels from my dream. I slowly walked over to that angel and said, "Thank you guys for the protection. Can you let the fire department put out the flames now, and say thank you to God for me for His care."

I turned around and walked over to the fireman and told him they could spray the cars. The angels put their wings down, walked over to me and just stood next to me. I walked five feet away from Charles and stopped. The angels walked with me and stopped, too! They didn't surprise me. I looked at each of them and thanked them with a nod. They didn't say a thing.

Then I said, "Okay, I know you are here with me God, your angels are all over the place. For a minute a little girl saw them and started yelling, "Mommy there are angels around that lady over there!" Then I looked at the young girl. She was about five years old. Then I glanced around me and I saw nothing. There were no angels, no gold wings, and no swords. I shrugged my shoulders, pulled out my cordless phone and called information. I had to find out where to rent a car.

The policeman that helped us was pretty nice. He gave Charles and me a ride to La Crosse. He said, "I have a daughter in La Crosse to visit, anyway." We got in his vehicle, and he drove us to La Crosse. He dropped us off at the airport.

He told us funny stories. My favorite one was about the time he and his family and friends went out to eat. They were doing the pizza thing and he had one too many beers. He said he usually gets really inspired to do his cigarette trick when he was drinking. So, when we got to the airport, I asked him to do his cigarette trick. I told him that I hoped he didn't mind, even though he wasn't tipsy.

He said, "Watch the cigarette now." He flipped that cigarette to his mouth and I didn't even see it go from his hand to his mouth. One minute it was in his hand, then he hit his wrist and it popped to his mouth with the tobacco end facing me. I was impressed. We thanked him for the ride and the trick and he gracefully left. I thought he was a funny guy. He's the kind of police officer that brings meaning to "being human."

We waited for an hour before we could catch our flights to our destinations. Charles boarded his plane to Chicago and I took Norwest to Minneapolis. We hugged each other and promised to e-mail.

I arrived in Minneapolis about one o'clock in the afternoon. I took a taxi from the airport to my house. I got there and police cars were all over the place. I thought, oh no! Now what? I tried to have the taxi pull into the driveway, but an officer stopped him, told him to move the taxi along. So, I got out and gave him his tip. I tried to walk up my driveway, and the same police officer stopped me, again.

He said, "I'm sorry miss you can't go in there."

I said, "And, why not, sir?"

He said, "King Savitri is in there."

I got real excited, I said, "Dad's in my house!"

I tried to pass him and go into my house. He held on to my arm and said, "Are you his daughter?"

I looked at him, then said, "Of course I am, who do you think I am? I live here! Now let me go! I want to see my dad!"

I started to raise my voice a little. He was getting me mad. I wasn't in a good mood anyway. My thirty thousand-dollar Mitsubishi just went up in flames, and this police officer was pissing me off. He was still holding on to my arm, I said, "Can you let go of my arm?"

He said, "May I see your drivers license?"

I dug in my purse for my Minnesota driver's license. I angrily handed it to him. He looked at it, then gazed me over with his eyes as if he was having lunch. I hated that. Sometimes beauty had its down side, especially in emergencies. He gave me back my license, and apologized. He said, "I'm sorry, your Royal Highness. Let me escort you to the King."

Mmmm, I forgot that I was a real princess. At least that helped. He walked me through the door to the living room where Dad was sitting.

Dad had people all around him, causing a commotion. Dad saw me, got up, extended his arms and said, "Sonthy!"

I ran into his arms, gave him a big hug and said, "I haven't seen you for two years. Wow! Look at the mess you brought with you!"

I was very happy to see my dad, but something didn't seem right. Why would he take time to come and see me? He could have just asked me to come see him. So, I asked the question, "Dad, what are you doing in my house? Why did you come here? I could have easily come to see you. You have a country to run. Were you missing me and mom?"

"That's exactly why I'm here. You and mom." Then dad's chin started to quiver.

Oh, something wasn't right, I thought. "Where is mom? How come she's not here?"

Dad ordered everybody out of the room, except his personal security guards. He said, "Sonthy, please sit down. Mom is dead. She was shot while driving her car. She lived twenty-four hours before she died. I was at the hospital with her right before she left. She whispered something in my ear." Dad beckoned me with his indexed finger to come closer. He whispered something in my ear that mom told him.

"What the hell!" I started pacing back and forth. I was totally furious. I was crying; I was angry, I wanted to kill that man. I hated him from the beginning! Dad told me that when the ambulance brought her to the hospital, she kept saying the murderer's name over and over again. The nurses put it in their reports, also. Dad had the police run the name, but found nothing. There was no man by that name. There was no social security number. There was no other names or aliases. Dad and I decided that the Brotherhood Corporation was going to pay for this! They sent their fucking hitman to kill my mother, because I didn't sleep with some corporate asshole! I was so furious. The veins in my neck and forehead were bulging out. I was still pacing.

Reggie told my dad who the man was. He was the guy whose name mom kept repeating. I told dad who he was too. I was really pissed. I was still crying.

Reggie came and held me. He said, "Honey, I packed some of your stuff. We have to get out of here. The man in the black Porsche will be back. He'll be looking for you."

Dad agreed. Dad said, "Here is a special phone line directly to me. Call me as soon as you get safe. I will take care of arrangements."

Dad handed me a briefcase full of money. Reggie and I went to the bank and emptied our accounts. We loaded his car with everything we thought we would need. Then we were gone.

Reggie and I had been running for a week. I hated sleeping in his car. I had to do that because we were driving for hours. We wanted to go anywhere away from Minneapolis.

I called dad right away when I thought we were safe. We were in a camping resort out in some woods. We got a little log and cabin to sleep in. We rented it for a month. Reggie and I really didn't know how long we would be staying.

I called dad right away. Dad picked up the phone. "Hello, Honey. How are you holding up?"

I replied, "I'm a little tired, but we're okay. We drove north into Canada and found some farm that had a church retreat on it. But we're okay dad."

Dad continued, "We had a closed- casket and invited all her friends. We had a fake funeral and a burial at the cemetery by that mean man's church, you know the one who's wife worked at the bank. You know that cemetery where grandpa's buried. She is supposedly buried next to grandpa. But we secretly brought her here, to Patmos. The president helped us keep it out of the media. She is here and things went just fine."

I said, "Dad. I'm still angry."

There was a little pause on dad's end, and then he said, "Honey, you know I'm not good with consolations, but let's get their asses. Do you want to come for the burial? The country knows she is here."

"Most definitely yes, I do want to come."

Dad told me that he had a plan worked out. He wanted me to listen to it and give my input. We were going to bring the killer down and destroy the corporation. I gave him the address where we were. He sent one of those hovering fighter airplanes. The plane landed in the fields, away from the buildings. It was nighttime when the plane came. When we saw it fly by, we were supposed to light off those night flares, but I forgot, until he passed by the second time.

The pilot saw the flares and stopped right over us. I was kind of excited. This airplane was one of the newer ones, the kind that looked like a flying saucer from outer space. It was silver and very futuristic. It landed, we got in, and it hovered until it got high enough, then it went straight up until it got into outer space.

We looked down at the Earth. It was a big, beautiful, blue ball. I had never been in outer space. It was breathtaking. Everything was extremely peaceful out there. I almost forgot why I was up there.

I was so busy taking in the scenery. Suddenly, a light shone through the windows onto the aircraft's instrument panel. The pilot was a little surprised to see all that light. I followed it with my eyes, upward. The light created a spectacular rainbow tunnel.

Inside the tunnel stood my mother. She said, "Sonthy Dear..."

I looked very suspiciously at her. I said to the pilot and Reggie, "I think I'm having illusions. Being in outer space may have gotten me sick. Do you guys see that?"

Reggie said, "What? You mean, your mother standing there in the beam of light? Of course, I see her. I didn't only see her, but I heard her say 'Sonthy Dear...'"

Mom, continued, "Sonthy, Dear, I want you to understand when you come to my burial that I'm not there, I'm here."

I looked at the pilot, and said, "Did you hear that, too?"

The pilot said, "Shhh, your mother is talking, why do you keep interrupting?"

I said, "Oh, so you do hear her?"

The pilot said, "Would you just be quiet for a minute?"

I was hurt. I thought I was seeing things, but it was real. The pilot wasn't nice about it at all.

"Honey, Dear, are you paying attention? I said, I'm not in the casket. I'm up here. So don't be crying for me, or visiting me at the grave. Just talk in the air wherever you are and I'll hear you. God has a message for you. He says, 'Count the living, not the dead, and don't commune with the dead so long you forget to live.'

"Now I have a message for you. The boy, Reggie Wheat, sitting next to you, is a good man. Don't be afraid to marry him. Tell your dad that I love him. As for you, things will work out fine. Bye, Dear. See you in seventy years." She reached right through the windshield of the aircraft and touched my hands. I felt courage shoot into me that wasn't present before.

I saw her turn around, and walk underneath this giant pearl as it opened upward on it's own. There were huge, solid gold walls on either side of the pearl. Light came rushing out of the bottom of the slowly lifting pearl.

A man with long white hair came out to greet her. He said, "Hello, Mrs. Savitry. I am the Branch of David. I am the Morning Star. Welcome home." He took my mother's hand. As He reached out, I saw holes in His hands. He then escorted her into the light. They eventually faded into the light.

Now I understood what they meant by "Pearly Gates." I always thought the "Pearly Gates" were like two gates that came together with a bunch of pearls on vertical bars like Graceland. I didn't think the "Pearly Gates" would be as large as the State of Minnesota!

The light vanished with a big lightning crack. There was silence and peace like there was before. I looked at Reggie and the pilot. They said, "We heard and saw everything."

Reggie said, "Did you see the holes in that guys hands?"

The pilot said, "Who is the Branch of David? Anybody know?"

Reggie and I smiled at each other and grinned silently. I said, "Don't you guys tell anyone. Just keep it to yourselves. Is that clear?"

They both nodded. I was appeased. I didn't want people thinking I was some spiritual yuppy. Shit! I didn't even go to church.

The aircraft descended when the earth rotated enough to see Patmos. We descended until my stomach went in my throat. I was vividly scared! The whole bottom of the craft turned bright white. It was going through the atmosphere with incredible speed. The pilot maneuvered the craft like it was his bicycle that he had been riding for years. He made a vertical landing behind my father's mansion. The trip was slightly more eventful for my blood, but perhaps another hundred more trips like that and I would be used to it. Maybe I should have been an astronaut.

When we got out of the plane, dad and his flock of servants were there to greet Reggie and me. The skies were bright and sunny. The air was mildly windy and warm. The island was surrounded with the beautiful Mediterranean. Our stay was brief. Dad didn't want to put his people at risk.

We had a private dinner with dad, Reggie and me. The food was excellent. Dad explained the plan to me. My main part was to contact dad, once I was positioned, to execute phase one. Dad's people around the world would carry out phase two. So, dad showed me the command center where all the activities would take place. I met the Chief of Security who would be in charge of the operation. After dinner and discussing the plan, we went to bed early because the next day we had to bury mom.

The next day came fast. The burial was very private. Dad wanted to make sure the whole ordeal was finished before he introduced me to his plan. I remembered what mom told me in the vision. I told dad about the entire vision after dinner. He and I went for a walk on the beach and conversed. We had about fifteen security guards in front of us and behind us, but we still had a nice walk. Burying mom wasn't as painful as I thought it would be. That vision really healed a lot in me.

When it was time to go, Reggie and I hugged dad goodbye and got on that crazy aircraft. The craft took off vertically, then went straight up with the nose pointing towards the stars like the Space Shuttle Columbia.

I was happy dad had this type of technology at his disposal. But, dad had always been into high-tech stuff. You should have seen the whole country. Everything was high-tech. Dad told me how much he had modernized the country in two years. He did a wonderful job. Going into outer space the second time wasn't quite as bad. Actually, I kind of liked being out there. Getting out there was going to take some time to get used to.

The aircraft landed at the farm quietly in the night. We waited until the orbit was just right. We said our good-byes to the pilot, and in a blink, the lights of the aircraft vanished into the night.

When we got back to the log cabin, the place was ransacked. I was glad I took the money and the laptop with me. They just destroyed most of our clothes. They didn't mess with the car, but I told Reggie to check it to make sure there wasn't any bomb or anything out of the ordinary. I had him check for bugging and anything that would look fishy, but the vehicle was clean.

We took off that night. We did not want to take any chances. We couldn't afford to be caught by The Brotherhood, Inc. I called the command center to inform them that they may initiate the Satellite Tracking Units. Reggie and I had already placed the belts they gave us around our waist. The belts helped dad's satellites track us. He could help us whenever we needed it. The little lights on the belts turned on. We were set to go.

We got in Reggie's sports utility vehicle, and went on highway thirty-five W south. We had to get back to Minneapolis fast. Dad configured a special device that would help us locate police officers with a simple button on my laptop. I plugged the laptop into the lighter and started to work on our plan. Reggie drove like a mad man. We were averaging between ninety and a hundred miles per hour. I liked these electronic fuzz- busters. They made rapid traveling easy.

We finally got back to the house. We went inside and took all our hidden samples along with the entire freezer and put it in the back of the vehicle. It looked like somebody had fun in the house, then they cleaned it up to make it look like nothing happened.

We got what we needed and began setting up the computers and equipment we needed to download the mainframe of The Brotherhood Corporation. We waited until night and we used Reggie's keys to get into the secured data area. We sprayed the cameras with black ink. When we finally got inside, Reggie took one computer and I sat at another. It took us about a half-hour before I could install the special disk Dad had given me to help download the information. Then I put in the right codes that I found in a file on the mainframe. We were ready. I started the downloading process. This would take all night, but we would have the entire copy of their mainframe by morning.

When we were finished hooking things up, we got out of there "ASAP." We safely got back to the vehicle. I climbed on the roof of the vehicle and turned on the black mobile satellite dish that dad created. I called dad on my cell phone and told him to do it!

I was excited now. Those bastards were going to see how pissed off I really was. We drove to a building a couple of blocks from The Brotherhood building and took turns sleeping. Reggie slept first, while I monitored the downloading process. It had been an hour and we already had ten percent of the mainframe. Things were going smoothly.

I woke Reggie up at three o'clock in the morning. He took over and I went to sleep. By the time Reggie woke up, the laptop had downloaded seventy percent.

The Brotherhood computer employees were stupid. You think they would have had people working at night in the mainframe areas. Mainframes didn't need major supervising. Of course, nobody had ever tried to steal their information, either.

Everybody was so afraid of the evil empire. I was still angry over mom's death. I was going to make sure that her death wasn't in vain. I just could not understand why a corporation would want to bring masses of people into the world just for body parts. Then wait until their organs were ready for harvesting. They harvested these people like cattle. I was absolutely furious. I thought I was going to work for a company that I would be proud of. I wanted to contribute something to society, not kill people. I felt like I had failed my mother, but not for long. We would see who was going to rise to power after I finished copying their mainframes.

Reggie woke me up at six. I was totally out. He had a grin on his face. I could tell he was pleased with our work. Once I was clearly awake, I asked him, "What's that grin about?"

He said, "Their mainframes have been completely downloaded and copied. Your father e-mailed me, just a little while ago, to tell me that they were currently in the process of copying a million CDs, half of which will be shipped to the FBI by tomorrow evening. He said that the other half would be shipped to the following address. He said his people would take care of things, just make sure you're safe."

"So, young lady, let's break things down and get some food." I was pleased. We ate some breakfast at some little café. I called dad.

I said to Reggie, "Reggie, dad's going to send a Lear Jet to pick up all the equipment at the Minneapolis International Airport at one o'clock in the afternoon." Reggie thought that was a good idea. I said, "Let's get rid of all this stuff and repaint your vehicle red or white, something other than green. Let's get some fake license plates made and then get out of the metro area, get a hotel and get some sleep."

It was nine o'clock in the morning and we had some hours to kill. We went driving all over the metro area, sight- seeing. We couldn't afford to leave all that equipment in the vehicle.

One o'clock came and we got the stuff loaded along with all our specimens, and video evidence. I was happy. It was only a matter of keeping away from these goons until the FBI reviewed the information. Let's lock all these boys up for good, I thought.

We drove from the airport and headed south towards Rochester. We got to Rochester, got a hotel room and got some really sweet sleep. The next day when I woke up, I felt like I had risen to power. Now I had the upper hand. My question was, how long were they going to take to find out that we gave their mainframe to the FBI? Ha, ha, ha. Life was feeling a little better. I felt like I was in control of my life again.

Chapter 6

Across Country

Rochester, Minnesota seemed like a nice town. I thought it was pretty. We drove through it until we stopped at our little motel. We got some burgers, ate and watched *Terminator Two* on cable. That night we slept good. It was about four thirty in the morning when my bladder woke me up. I had to go pretty bad. Reggie was still sleeping. I had just finished peeing.

There was a loud bang, boom, bang on the bathroom door. I yelled, "ieek!" and abruptly leaped off the commode. I yelled, "What is it?"

Reggie said, "You got to get out of there! They are here!" I heard a helicopter and as I came out of the bathroom, I saw the light from the head light of the helicopter shine into the room. Suddenly, there was a spray of bullets across the window shattering glass across the bed. Reggie grabbed my hands and we dove onto the floor. My heart was racing. Reggie got out his Silver gun with the silencer. Bullets were still spraying across the bed, the inner walls, and onto the table. Bullets were shattering lamps and mirrors everywhere in the motel room. Reggie periodically placed his hands on the bed along with the gun, pointed his gun at the black helicopter and let off a couple of rounds.

I shouted, "Do you have another gun?!"

He replied, "No, but you got to stay down, crawl to the door and open it. See if there are any more of them outside!"

I crawled under the table and then to the door. I opened it, and everybody in the hotel was screaming, running to their cars, and driving away. I looked for our vehicle, grabbed my purse and the keys, and ran for it. I jumped into the Explorer and honked the horn. Reggie let off a couple more rounds and ran to the truck. The minute he got inside, I squealed the tires and raced off into the sunrise.

Things were quiet for about five minutes. I looked through my rear view mirror and that black helicopter was gaining three blocks behind us. He was quickly on top of us.

Reggie yelled, "Faster! Faster!" I thought it was pointless. We couldn't outrun a helicopter.

I yelled back, "Shoot the damn thing's back rudder!"

Reggie stuck his face out the window and sprayed some bullets at the passengers. The thing came down closer to the vehicle. Reggie said, "They're lowering some rope. There is a guy coming down the rope. Do something!?"

The helicopter noises drowned out his voice, but he yelled louder. I started to swerve the vehicle side to side so the guy wouldn't land on the roof. I was swerving to the left and the helicopter moved three feet to the right. They let off some shots that went into the side of the door. Reggie shot at the guy hanging on the rope. It was a direct hit right in his heart. He dropped to the pavement like lead. He lay there, presumably dead. The helicopter kept pursuing us.

They decided to change their strategy. They dropped down a bunch of ropes with hooks on them. The hooks grabbed the back of the Explorer and hoisted it up. Our back end went upward as the wheels lifted off the pavement. The vehicle was swaying in the air. The front end was ten feet off the ground and I was on my edge. Oh God. How was I going to get out of this? I thought.

Reggie kept shooting. I was totally helpless. The helicopter dragged us in the air across some farmland for two miles. I said to Reggie, "Did you hear what I said? Shoot the rudder! The rudder!"

He finally understood me. The helicopter's fluttering noise was so loud my ears were starting to hurt. Reggie loaded five rounds into the back end of the helicopter. I heard some loud crackling noises. The helicopter started spiraling downward with smoke coming from the engine. Reggie finally got those idiots.

Oh shit! The ground was rising to meet us fast! We descended into a harvested cornfield. First, the nose of the Explorer hit the ground. My head went forward with a jerk that left my neck aching. Reggie slammed into the dashboard because he didn't have his seat belt on; he was busy shooting.

After the front end landed, the rear end landed on its wheels. I immediately stepped on the gas. The tension on the chains increased and finally snapped off the Explorer. I saw the helicopter crash on its belly with a loud explosion. We felt it under our seats. The whole thing went up in flames. We kept driving through the cornfields until we got back on the highway. I sighed a sigh of relief, once again. We drove to Madison, Wisconsin and rented a hotel room. We were safe for the time being, but who knew for how long.

In the hotel room, we rested, and took our separate showers. Then we got some food from the restaurant across the street. We ate inside. I didn't feel like entertaining company or speaking to anybody, so Reggie and I locked ourselves in the hotel room for the rest of the night. We slept like babies that night. The night was too short. I felt like I needed more sleep.

Reggie was already up and dressed when I got up. He was sitting by the window with his gun in his right hand. When he heard me get up, he put his gun away and sat by the side of the bed next to me. He said, "Good morning, sleepy head."

I groggily said, "Morning."

He continued to say, "I got us some blueberry pancakes for breakfast, I'll set up while you get ready to eat."

I slowly got up. My neck was still hurting. It was a little better than yesterday. I went to the bathroom, did my thing, and came out to the eating area. We sat down to eat our food. The blueberry pancakes were very good. They reminded me of mom's pancakes. I quickly got the thoughts of mom out of my head. We quickly ate, cleaned up, and took the keys to the lobby. We were on the road again.

We repainted the vehicle in Madison. We were happy with the job. Our destination was Chicago, but we were going through Milwaukee first. Reggie had some connections he wanted to get a hold of. We arrived in Milwaukee about one o'clock in the afternoon.

Reggie used my phone to call his friends. We got a hold of his friends. We bought some guns and ammunition from them. We also bought a brown camouflage painted Humvee. We got three M16s, two 357 Magnums, a hundred grenades, one machine gun, two Bazookas (missile launchers), some plastic explosives, four computerized Scud Missile Projectiles, some micro cameras, a military tent, five knives, and one helicopter, painted like brown seaweed. Finally, we bought one semi-truck with a trailer.

The helicopter and the semi-truck were kept in a warehouse in Industrial Park. We were going to take them out as we went, at least until dad could put Sister Earth into action, or before war broke out. We drove to the warehouse and loaded the ammunition into the helicopter. I was glad his friends were up and up. We attached the tarp over the helicopter. The helicopter was on a trailer, so we attached it to the Humvee and drove both of them into the semi-truck. I got in the Explorer and drove it into the semi also.

We got in the semi and drove to a truck stop. There, we bought a bunch of food and put it in the large cooler in the back. We changed into our camouflage gear. I put on my military hat and we were off to Sioux Falls, South Dakota. Mom's Grandmother was part Sioux Indian. I had some relatives in the Sioux Tribe. Dad called them and they were ready for us.

I bet those Brotherhood creeps were scrambling, trying to find us now. When dad called, he asked us to turn on CNN. I turned on the small t.v. in the cab to CNN. There was a representative from the FBI that said that they were investigating the Brotherhood, Inc. for murder and genetic crimes. He said that he had received copies of the Brotherhood's mainframe from an unknown source and that it was sufficient evidence for indictment. The investigation was still pending.

As soon as I heard that, I was very happy. I knew this meant total war for Reggie and me. We drove faster. Reggie and I had gotten a little closer. Since we had such a long drive, we got to know each other better. I found out what R.W. did at the company. He worked for the Brotherhood, Inc. as the Chief Director of Information Services. He had keys to every building and access to very high level information.

He said, "They will certainly put a price on my head. By the way, what was it that your mother told your dad before she left?"

As soon as he said, "Your mother," a bomb went off inside me. I became that much more determined to destroy The Brotherhood, Inc. I was instantly angry. I took a short breath, then a deep one, and counted to ten. I said with a stern voice, "I would appreciate if you don't mention my mom for a while, for a long while."

I looked at him with mixed emotions, angry, lonely, hurt, sad, and frustrated. I didn't want to feel the pain. All I knew was that I almost forgot the pain was there. I was excited that the FBI got the information. I was anxious to get to Sioux Falls, but my mood was a little ruined. I was silent for about a half an hour after that. All I could hear was the humming of the tires, the engine, and the wind passing by my rolled down window.

Thoughts went through my mind. I had flashbacks of the time dad took us up to our cabin on the lake, and mom and I had fun swimming and splashing all around. I had thoughts of the many bike races we had, racing through our neighborhood. Mom always let me win. I had thoughts of late- night girl talks and early morning Saturday cooking. I had thoughts of things that started to swell tears in my eyes.

I started to softly cry. Tears were pouring down both my cheeks. I started breathing with short choppy breaths. I had to get out of the truck. I had to get some air! I said, "Reggie could you pull over to the side, please?"

He said, "Will that do?" The moment the truck stopped, I bolted out of the cab and sprinted like a wild mustang, five blocks ahead of the truck wailing at the top of my lungs.

I was walking in circles in the middle of the empty freeway, pulling at my hair, shaking both my fist to God in the sky, jumping up and down, cussing and swearing and finally, beating the open air with my fist. I was confused, and disoriented. When

I got to the end of my rope, I just collapsed onto my knees right there on the side of the freeway. I guess my mother's death was still sore with me. It just hit me out of the blue!

I didn't know it, but Reggie was running behind me, yelling, "Sonthy! Sonthy! Hey Sonthy! Get down! The airplane! The airplane! It's shooting at you. Get down!" He ran behind me and tackled me to the ground as the plane shot bullets past us. We quickly got up and made a mad rush for the truck. The plane was flying low again. It flew past us and sprayed bullets at our feet. Dirt jolted up into our faces.

We ran to the back of the truck and opened the large white double doors. I grabbed the M16 and shot some rounds at the aircraft. Reggie got a Bazooka and loaded it with a projectile. He flipped the scope up on the top of the thing. The airplane made a bank and headed for us again. It was flying very low. I could see the guy pointing his guy at us. There were two of them: the pilot and the assassin.

As the plane came by, I shot the front window on the pilot's side. The glass shattered. I didn't know if I got the pilot or not, but the plane went out of control. At the time the plane went out of control, Reggie shot the projectile. The plane was flying too low by now. Reggie couldn't have missed it. It was a direct hit right into the cab. The thing exploded right above us. We climbed in the trailer to get away from the falling debris. Burning fragments of the airplane fell around us. There was a charred fleshly smell in the air. The kind that was sour and made me feel like vomiting. I saw limbs and burnt body parts splatter against the trailer. We quickly shut the doors and jumped in the semi and started cruising.

We were both overjoyed! We slapped each other's hands, and yelled Wooo! Hooo! I was definitely in a better mood. I grinned and I was shaking my head up and down saying, "Oh, yea! Oh yea! Oh yea!"

I looked at Reggie, then said, "She said, it was Mr.Zum. It was Mr. Zum."

Reggie said, "What are you talking about?"

I replied, "The last thing mom said, was 'It was Mr. Zum that shot me. It was Mr. Zum that shot me.'"

Reggie, turned and looked into the road as if he was seeing some ghost. He said, "I figured it was him! That asshole!" For the first time, I saw serious emotions on Reggie's face.

He always seemed so calm about everything. Reggie had one of those strong spirits. He clenched his jaw and grinded his teeth. I said, "Reggie, ease up on your teeth. I like your smile."

He quickly looked at me, and stopped grinding and clenching his teeth. He continued driving. I put a CD in the CD player and cranked up the music. I wasn't about to let anything ruin my mood!

I called dad. Dad answered, "What is it Sonthy?"

"Dad, an airplane just attacked us, but Reggie shot it down with the Bazooka. There were no survivors,"

Dad was pleased. He said, "Keep up the good work, I expect no less from you. Let's keep our honor."

I calmly replied, "Dad, we'll be coming into Sioux Falls in about an hour, can you let your people know we have all the supplies?"

"Sure thing, Honey. Here is the next thing I want you to do. Have Reggie leave a copy of the master keys to all buildings, and to the warehouses where there are no people working. Then, when I'm ready, I'll e-mail you. Keep your computer on. After you read the e-mail, press the 'enter' button. Make sure it is two o'clock tomorrow morning when you press the 'enter' button. And by the way, don't forget to turn on CNN for the noon report. We are going into phase two once you get to Sioux Falls. Call me after you watch the news. Bye now and be careful."

"Bye, dad."

We got to Sioux Falls on schedule. Jim Showfox and his crew took us to the sight out in the middle of the desert. Mr. Showfox was in charge of operation phase two. We arrived there about ten o'clock in the night. The place was busy. Dad had some serious connections. Kim Whitehead was there. He was the

FBI agent who worked along with Sandy Windworth, the CIA agent.

Mr. Showfox's people set up our tent. It was a small compound, but it sure had a lot of people. There were four satellite dishes on top of buildings. There were tents all over the place. It was a M.A.S.H.- type compound, except they also had buildings. Wow! Dad was serious! Yea! I was excited. I had adrenaline pumping through me.

Mr. Showfox and all the department heads called a conference meeting. We entered this room that had carpet and looked like a courtroom. There was shiny, light brown, glossy wood on all the walls. Mr. Showfox briefed us on the operation's objectives. The objective was to play cat and mouse. Reggie and I were the bait. The command center would coordinate with Reggie and I to destroy all enemy forces in mobilization and, at the same time, render their communication systems and their operation facilities useless. Any assassins were to be killed on site.

The meeting was over. It was one thirty in the morning. Reggie and I got some food and sat down to eat in the cafeteria. Everyone else was dismissed. We had to leave the next day. We couldn't afford to have this base found. The Brotherhood, Inc. was looking for Reggie and me, but they were going to find more then just us.

It was two o'clock in the morning. I called dad. Dad picked up the phone. He said, "We're ready. Thank Reggie for giving the keys. We completed the procedure. After you press the button, you got to get to Florida, but take the long route that Mr. Showfox gave you. Keep those belts on. Keep up the good work. Bye, Honey"

I said my good-byes and hung up. Then I opened my e-mail and read it. Oh, boy! Dad was really going to make a splash. I pressed the 'enter' button and closed my e-mail. Reggie and I went to our quarters and slept great. It was eight in the morning when Reggie and I woke up.

We woke up to the sound of military trucks rolling by our window. We got up and dressed. There was a knock on the door. It was Sandy Windworth. She and Kim Whitehead wanted us to join them for breakfast. They wanted to go over a few things with us before we left.

We got our breakfast from the mess hall and sat down to eat. They briefed us and gave us some documents to study. The new President, George W. Bush, Jr. signed a CIA document that made Reggie and me CIA agents. We were very happy to accept. We each got our special guns, materials, and identifications. We got our fingerprints and did all the necessary things that had to be signed. We said goodbye to Mr. Showfox, the project director, and everybody else. We got in our Ford Explorer and off we went. I brought the little television from the semi-truck. I had to watch CNN to see what dad did.

I turned on CNN. There was a commercial on. I waited for a couple of minutes until the commercial was over. Another commercial came on about condoms. I thought it was funny. They had millions of white animated sperms, dressed in camouflage, as soldiers, storming an ocean beach. They had hundreds of amphibious vehicles dropping these soldiers into the water. The soldiers stormed the beach only to find themselves smashing their faces against a long and high invisible barrier that was placed a hundred yards inland. The rest of the soldiers who were not paying much attention rear-ended the other soldiers in a massive pile against the invisible barricade. The commercial showed a profile of the wall with the soldier's faces meshed against it. Their hands, noses and cheeks slightly indented the wall. Then the name of the condom company came slamming onto the screen with a loud bang, like somebody was slamming a large steel vaulted door. My favorite part was the well-orchestrated military "action adventure" music that enveloped the whole scene. It gave the whole thing a dramatic effect. The commercial was well done and very clever.

Finally, the anchorwoman came on. She said, "Leading the afternoon news is the Brotherhood, Inc., Genetic Research and

Organ Transplant Company. The company had a hundred and fifty warehouses around the country bombed this morning. The company spokesperson said that it did a hundred and ninety million dollars of damage. Previous FBI investigation of the company is still pending. The two twin brothers who founded the company are not available for comments. Nobody was killed and only a few had minor injuries."

"Wow! Dad's serious, woo ho! Yes!" I shouted.

Reggie listened quite intensely. He had a very satisfied composure while driving. I, on the other hand, went ballistic!

We left Sioux Falls in a good mood. We headed down Interstate 29. We cranked up the tunes. Now I can sing pretty well. But Reggie, on the other hand, sang like a couple of cows, and some goats shooing roaches from the barn. He was so cute singing that he made the whole singing experience rather amusing.

The phone rang. I picked it up and said, "Hi, dad! Great job!"

He replied, "Thanks, but I don't have much time. I sent some helicopters to take your Explorer to your next destination in Kansas City, Missouri. The helicopters dropped off two black motorcycles. Some Brotherhood men are on your trail. They'll be reaching you in about an hour. Get on the bikes and ride down the center of the road in the next hour. Make sure to stay on the yellow line, no matter what. When you get to Kansas City, give me a call. Bye." I hung up.

We turned onto Interstate 70. We found the motorcycles with the helicopters waiting. They loaded up the Explorer into the big double bladed one, and off they went.

Immediately we started riding on the yellow middle line, one behind the other. I was leading. We were about to the spot dad told us. Dad had people dig a giant hole in the street and cover it with a painted tarp so it looked like the road. It blended in very well. Then, they stretched it over the road so that from a distance you could not tell the difference. I heard some gun shots behind me. I looked in my mirrors. I saw two black sports utility vehicles with tinted windows on our asses. We were just about to the giant hole. There was a road marker that was put on both sides of the road to warn us. The signs said, "Middle Road Lane 1 mile." We drove on the middle line. We were going ninety miles per hour. I could hear bullets whistling by my ears. I didn't dare look back. In a split second we crossed over the hole. The two trucks fell into the hole. In the hole, dad put some explosives. The minute the two trucks hit bottom, off they went with a ground-shaking explosion.

We skidded to a stop when we heard the deafening explosion. We turned around and saw the hole. Large flames violently expressed themselves inside the pit. We drove back to the sight, looked into the flame for a couple of minutes, and off we went to Kansas City, Missouri. We got there on schedule. We located the garage where we were supposed to find our white Explorer. There it was. We exchanged the bikes for the truck. We immediately were on our way.

I called dad. Dad answered, "Hello, Sonthy. How did it go?"

I replied, "It worked out very well. How come we had to drive in the center of the road?"

Dad spoke again and said, "We put a steel beam under the tarp that was just wide enough for your tires, but not for a car."

"Hey, that was pretty good, dad. Do you sit around thinking of these things, dad?"

Dad said, "No, Honey. My people do. I'll call you when I'm ready. Bye."

I said my good-byes and hung up. We headed to St. Louis, Missouri.

The other phone rang. I said, "Hello."

The familiar voice said, "Your not going to get away you little shit! I'll find you and feed your flesh to my pigs."

I replied, "Not if I feed your flesh to my pigs first, Mr. Zum!" I quickly pushed the "hang up button" with my right index finger.

The same phone rang again; I picked it up. "Hello" I said.

A pleasant friendly male voice said, "Hello, this is Mr. Showfox. How are you guys holding up?"

I said, "Not too bad. What is it?"

He quickly continued, "We've picked up an aircraft heading your direction. I'm sending you one of our stunt pilots to pick you up right there in the street. Move your vehicle to the side so she can land. She said she couldn't land because your Explorer was in the way. Goodbye."

Mr. Showfox hung up. For a minute there I thought it was the Zum Scum. We pulled our vehicle to the side. I heard the Cessna land. It was Sandy Windworth! She motioned us to get into the plane. We fumbled into the airplane. In the matter of a minutes, we were in the air.

She was very good at flying this thing. She did a bank and headed somewhere I didn't know. My stomach went to my throat. I asked, "Where are we going?"

Sandy replied, "To the Colorado Mountains. We have something planned for these pilots flying behind us." Reggie and I both spun around to look back.

Oh no! It was Mr. Zum's clowns. There was a black, twin-engine airplane behind us. It wasn't right on our tail, but it was just close enough to make me nervous. How was a girl supposed to get any rest with so much commotion, twisting and turning, climbing, and diving.

I felt my stomach in my esophagus when we did the upside down loop, "Uug! Help! I think I'm going to puke."

Reggie opened one of the windows and I vomited out the window. A disgusting colorful gunk of undigested food flew away in a stream. Reggie pulled out his pocket-handkerchief and handed it to me. I quickly wiped my face. I did not think I had any more food left in my stomach. Small airplanes and I did not get along. I loved flying, though. When I was up very high, things did not bother me that much.

I went to the back to sit next to Reggie. Reggie held my hand. I felt much better after throwing up.

The plane behind us was closing in. Suddenly, Sandy took the plane into a seven-minute dive. My eyes got real big. Reggie wasn't bothered by it. He usually was not bothered by much. He kept himself very calm in most situations.

Sandy handled the plane like I handled my toothbrush. She did a turning spin downward. I clearly saw that there were three black airplanes chasing us. We continued to dive. I was beyond fear now because the ground was coming fast! We were heading towards a farm that had two silos. Sandy pulled up on her wheel and banked left right before she hit the ground. She flew between the silos as she was banking left, woo! Now that scared me! I thought we were going to be part of those silos, for sure!

The plane that was immediately behind us couldn't pull up in time and crashed to the ground headfirst. What a bright red, violent explosion! Airplane pieces flew into the air with dirt and debris like an emotional twister. As we banked left, we did a complete circle. We headed back, the same direction we came from. The second plane didn't make it between the silos. It tried to bank, but it was too late. Both wings caught the two silos right in the middle and the wings tore off like velcro! The plane ended up in the cornfields. It, too, went up in a crackling, sizzling blaze! Oh yes! I was beginning to enjoy this stunt flying too much! Ho ho! Yea! Woo wee! We wove to the left and to the right. We went up and down. We did loops, dives, and banks. Finally, we flew between trees and radio towers and still, we couldn't shake the last pilot. He was good. They kept on shooting at us. We climbed to twenty five hundred feet.

We were now in Colorado. We flew between the Rocky Mountains. My phone rang. I picked it up. "Hello," I said.

There was a slow, calm male voice. He said, "This is Kim Whitehead, Ms. Windworth's partner. May I speak to her?"

I replied, "Yes." I handed the phone to Sandy. Sandy took the phone and said, "Aha, yea, aha, aha, ok." Then she handed the phone back to me.

I put the phone to my ear, then I said, "Yes."

Mr. Whitehead continued, "We took your Explorer to Macon, Georgia. Albert Pederson will assist you when Sandy lands the airplane. Right now, just enjoy the show. There is something coming up in five minutes. So, relax, if you need anything, just call. Bye." He hung up.

We climbed higher. We had to put on some oxygen masks. The mountains were gorgeous. The clouds were white and billowing. The snow was sparkling white. It was exciting! There was a narrow passage that we had to go between. The airplane had to tip its wings sideways, in the vertical position. As we were coming through the narrow strip with sharp hungry rocks on both sides, ready to devour our plane, we banked right to clear the area. I was very impressed. Sandy, our pilot, was very skilled. We made it very easily. As we banked and rose higher, I saw a man on one side of the narrow strip shoot a steel net across the strip, which unraveled as it stuck into the other side. It was a large tube that shot out like a rocket. The steel net quickly fell down in time for the black airplane to run into it like black widow's web. The plane quickly burst into flames. A big cloud of steam and smoke went up and blended into the mountains gentle clouds.

We continued to fly to our destination: Macon, Georgia. We stopped at some small airport to refuel before we started our journey to Macon. Things went smoothly all the way to Macon. I was very pleased with Sandy's flying. Reggie and I let Sandy know how pleased we were with her abilities. She appreciated the gratitude, but she didn't have much to say. For her, it was just another day of stunt flying.

We arrived in Macon, Georgia safely. We took a taxi to Albert's place. He was pleased to see us. He was a little over-zealous, if you asked me. He said, "It is my pleasure to finally meet you, your Royal Highness!" That royal stuff was for the birds, but I played along.

When we got in the Explorer, Reggie made fun of me. He said, "It's a pleasure to want you, your Royal Be-highness!" I busted out laughing. He made this funny face and wagged his head side to side like a dog's tail. He was too much!

Reggie quickly looked into the mirrors. He abruptly pulled the vehicle to the side and loaded his gun. Then he placed his silencer on it. I watched him. I immediately followed and loaded my gun. Reggie was like a hawk. He noticed small abnormal things that communicated to him that something was wrong. His senses were very sharp. He flowed very well with his intuition. Something was wrong. He was acting a little funny again. It was like animals acting funny before a storm.

I was slowly using my intuition, also. I was beginning to just do it and think later. Something definitely was wrong, but I couldn't put my hands on it. Reggie got out of the Explorer in the middle of Interstate 75. He held his gun out with both hands. I sat in the SUV and didn't move a muscle.

"What the hell is going on!" I yelled.

Reggie put his index finger to his lips and said "shhhh."

Reggie continued to walk around the car, cautiously. His gun was still pointed, using both arms. He had his legs slightly spread out, shoulder length. His back was leaned up against the SUV. He slowly bent down and pointed the gun under the SUV. He moved it from side to side. He motioned me to get in the driver's side. I quickly moved over. The vehicle was still running. He cautiously worked his way around the vehicle to the passenger side. There was nothing there. He put his gun back in its holster next to his side. He got in, then quickly motioned me to go.

There was a thud on the roof as soon as I moved the vehicle. He motioned for me to quickly put on the brakes. I brought the vehicle to a screeching halt. A person rolled down the windshield and onto the hood, then fell in front of the vehicle. Reggie quickly pulled out his gun, and angrily slammed the passenger door open with his body. He carelessly left the door open. He was like a hostile cheetah, protecting his cubs.

He swiftly ran around to the front of the SUV and with one swift move, he pointed the gun at an old woman clumsily lying on the pavement. As she got up, to her surprise, she discovered a silver gun in her face! He got up close and pointed the gun at her forehead. I looked a little closer at the thin, frail figure. It was that old rag woman that I ran into a couple of times earlier. The really strange old lady that said stuff I couldn't understand.

I slowly got out of the SUV and walked over to them. "Reggie! Put the gun down! I know her!" I bellowed.

Reggie interrogated her. He said, "What were you doing on our roof? Who sent you? Who's your superior?"

I told him, "Look Reggie, she is harmless. But keep an eye on her. I have a few questions of my own to ask her."

I went up to her and said, "Why were you in my driveway? What do you want with me?"

She didn't say a thing for a minute. All three of us were standing there, quietly waiting for one or the other to speak. She finally spoke and said, "Put wetness to your water and let not the sun rise upon the dew, for they are lost souls which betroth their heart to the air. Resurrect the Sleepers, I say!"

Reggie grabbed her arm, then got in her face and said, "What the hell does that mean?"

She softly replied, "Judgement first before hell is cast into the Lake of Fire. Then will the brethren upon many stars dwell in unity!" As soon as she said that, we looked at each other to try to make a connection with the words, but we were utterly confused.

When we looked up, Reggie and I were standing alone. Reggie's fingers were gripping the air. Reggie looked at me, annoyed by the situation, shook his head side to side, walked over to the driver's side of the vehicle, and grunted. He got in forcibly and slammed the door. He waited until I got in, then drove away on Interstate 10, towards Jacksonville, Florida. Reggie was silent for the rest of the drive.

It was three o'clock in the morning when we got to Jacksonville, Florida. Neither one of us spoke the whole trip. All I could hear was the humming of the tires on the road and that little old lady's words going around in my head, saying, "Resurrect the Sleepers! Resurrect the Sleepers!" There was something thick in the air inside the vehicle, but we never discussed the old woman.

We rented a hotel room in downtown Jacksonville. We slept like babies that night. The morning came quickly. I slowly got out of bed. My muscles were aching. I needed a good hot tub and a massage. We took turns using the bathroom. I went in first. I did my thing, and Reggie went in and did his. We got dressed. Every morning, when I got dressed, I always put on the belt that dad gave me. It had the red emergency button on it. If I pressed it, dad would know that I needed some serious help. He would use his satellites to track my position and then send in the troops. When I pressed the red buttoned, it was supposed to automatically dial the mini cell phone on my belt. The microphone was supposed to pick up every audible noise and send it to dad. I had never had to use it yet, but I was sure I would.

We got our suitcases and started to walk out the door. Reggie opened up the door. We stepped into the hallway to walk to the elevator. The minute we both stepped into the hall, there were five guns pointed at us. The men were all wearing dark suits and ties. They all had silencers on their guns. Reggie and I didn't move a muscle, except for my little fingers. I immediately pressed the emergency button on my belt.

My heart was beating like pistons in an engine. My adrenaline was ready to kick some ass! Reggie motioned to me to do nothing. I could see some of these men's coldness. They were sheer killing machines. Mr. Zum Man and his goons surrounded us. The minute I saw Mr. Zum Man, anger rose in me, like red lava, spraying into the air. But I didn't move a muscle. My legs froze. I thought I was dead, for sure.

Mr. Zum Man walked over to Reggie and cracked him in the jaw with the butt of his piece. A little blood slightly ran down the edge of Reggie's lower lip. Some more hot lava sprayed into my chest. My face was beginning to turn red from the heat of my anger. I was so angry, I decided that this bald-headed pig must die!

He walked over to me. He stopped an inch from my face. He stuck out his long bumpy tongue and licked my right cheek with one long, lizard- like sweep. It was the most disgusting thing I had ever experienced! His spit felt like tiny little black demons slowly slithering on my cheeks. It was green, foamy saliva that fell onto my chest. I frowned at his barbaric behavior. I took a quick glance at the green spit.

I said to him, "You take pleasure in torture, but I'll take pleasure in killing you."

He quickly slapped my face without moving. He was still an inch from me. He barked back at me, like a ferocious Doberman, "I tell you when to speak, you warm piece of carcass!"

I took a deep breath. He walked around me, like a dog sniffing a fresh pile of brown dung. This man had no concept of life. His value on life was that it was pleasing to terminate.

When he finished walking around me, he told his men to "move out." I hated his deep raspy voice. When he spoke, his breath smelled like puke! They surrounded us like a fortified brick wall. They quietly lead us out of the hotel and into their black vehicles.

The Zum Man made me sit in his black Mercedes while Reggie sat with the other goons in their black BMW's. We paraded out of there like a buffalo stampede; tires screamed, engines ground, and pure evil led the way. For the first time in my life, I was actually afraid. I could feel Reggie. He seemed to be afraid, too. Reggie wasn't afraid of much, but Mr. Zum gave him reasons to be afraid. He never wanted to discuss it. We drove for hours. Mr. Zum did not say a word.

We finally reached some warehouse in the middle of nowhere. I didn't know where I was. They led us into the warehouse. It was large, empty and chilly. The ceiling had steel beams running across it, and long florescent lights, in every direction. All the cars pulled inside and made a large circle.

Then Mr. Zum Man got out of his car. He motioned for me to get out. I got out and walked around to his side of the vehicle.

He had his gun out. All the other goons, one by one, stepped out of their cars and slammed their doors with a hard thud.

They brought two chairs and put them in the middle of the circle. Mr. Zum motioned for us to sit down on them. They didn't bother to tie us up. We weren't going anywhere.

There were so many of them! The men stood in a large circle, side by side. Suddenly, one of the large doors opened, and a long black limousine slowly came inside. The door closed. The limousine had tinted windows so we couldn't see inside. It stopped right behind Mr. Zum Man's Mercedes. Everybody stood still. Not even Zum Scum moved. The limousine's driver opened his door and came out. He cautiously walked over to the back door on the driver's side and slowly opened it. We watched to see who would come out. The whole mob of men watched. The door was opened for a half an hour. In that time nobody moved a muscle.

Finally some white shoes and a leg with white pants popped out. A very handsome middle- aged man dressed in a double-breasted white suit stood between the door. He smiled very brightly and said to the gentlemen, " It is a beautiful day."

Another foot came out, then another man walked out of the limousine that looked just like the other man, except, he was wearing a black pinstriped suit. I spoke under my breath, "Those two fucking bastards!"

They both strutted to Reggie and me. Even though Reggie and I were scared shitless, we weren't about to let them know. We made up our minds. We were warriors and that was the way it was going to stay. We never showed the slightest bit of fear. We would die with honor and dignity and we would live with honor and dignity.

The man in the black suit called one of his men over to him. Then he said to his man, "Give me your gun."

The man gave him his gun. Dylan pointed the gun at Reggie's head and held it for about five minutes. He thought and thought. Then he removed the gun from Reggie's head and pointed it at my head. He held it there. I started drifting into my memories. I knew I was dead anyway. He held the gun at my head for about a minute. Then he slowly pulled the trigger. The minute he pulled the trigger, I felt my body lift up in the air. I felt tingles all over my body. I was flying. I started to go past Mars, Jupiter, and then, there was that lit tunnel. I walked through it. As I got to the end, there was a bright light and the light blinded me. I couldn't see a thing. The only thing I could see was white, white, and white. Then I heard a calm steady voice say, "Do you always keep the safety on this thing?"

Well, that quickly brought me out of my daydreaming! Devin looked at Dylan and said, "May I?"

Dylan handed the silver, shiny gun to Devin. Devin walked over to his man and said, "My brother asked you a question, do you!?"

The man began to open his mouth to speak, but before he uttered a word Devin briskly shoved the silver piece into his mouth, undid the safety and off went the gun! The bullet went right through his mouth, through his white fleshy brain, out the back of his skull and into the chest of the tallest man behind him. They both dropped to the floor like two bowling balls. The first man was as dead as dead could be. The second man was not dead. He was on the ground, screaming in pain. My eyes somehow saw the bullet in slow motion as it spun and whisked though the air. Wow! I rubbed my eyes, just to make sure that I wasn't seeing things. Devin quickly let out a mimicking scream and ran to the man screaming and yelling on the ground, then shot him right in the heart.

All the men started whispering one to another in murmurs. Devin abruptly turned around and roared, "What!?"

Everybody was immediately silent. No one moved a muscle. Devin walked back to Dylan. Dylan was still standing in front of us.

Devin said, "I would love to torture you, Reggie. Just because you have been with us so long. Now this is a beauty. This is Dr. Sonthy Savitry. The bitch who is costing my company a little fortune-"

I forcefully interjected, "It's your mother who's the bitch, not me!" Then he slapped me. He slapped me so hard I fell off the chair. I quickly tucked my legs under my body, leaped straight up and stood upon my feet into my karate stance. As fast as I fell down, I stood up!

Dylan said, "Look Devin, we don't have time for this. We have a meeting in Europe pretty soon. Let's get going." Dylan looked at me and said, "My brother and I wanted to meet you before you were dead. Now we have."

I said, "I don't die easy. Maybe you didn't notice that yet?"

They frowned, cleared their throats and called Mr. Zum to them. All three of them walked over to the limousine, got inside and left.

As Mr. Zum was getting in the limousine, he told the men to kill us. Then we watched the limousine drive away.

As soon as the limousine was gone, all the men pulled out their guns. They were still in a large circle. They put their hands on all their pieces and pointed them at us. They all had perfect form. It was like a political execution. The leader of the goons started to count down from ten, nine, eight, seven, six, five... The minute he said, "five" an idea popped into my head.

I quickly stood up and started to take off all my clothes. I stripped, butt naked. The leader just stared at my breast and my super pubic area. I saw his eyes caressing my body like a cool wind as I stood there in my most seductive pose. Then he forgot to count. The rest of the men, one by one, put down their guns and slowly started walking towards us. When they got to us, the leader started to caress my breast with his large hands. Reggie cracked him a punch across his jaws. Three men piled on Reggie and held him still. The leader walked over to Reggie and punched him, extremely fiercely, in the gut. Reggie keeled over and started coughing.

I jumped between them. Then I said, "Hey, you don't have to fight over me. You can all have me one at a time before I die. If I'm going to die, won't you at least give me some pleasure before I go, big boys?"

One at a time, they all grunted, "Ah huh." I lowered my voice, squinted my eyes and put on a sexy grin.

I continued to say, as seductively as possible, "Which one of you has the largest penis?" They began to argue, one at a time. I saw they all had serious bulges in their pants. Wooo! I hoped I knew what I was doing. It was working so far. At least I was not dead. I had to buy some time before dad could bring some help. I continued to say, "Well, you all can't have sex with me with your pants still on. Can you, now?" They looked at each other and, one by one, they began to unzip their pants and take them off.

The leader started to rub his hands all over me. I was totally sickened. I felt like barfing. But I contained it. The men rushed to get in line. They made a perfect line behind each other. Then I said. "Isn't there an honor system between you boys? Aren't you warriors? I will only have sex with the strongest warrior. Whoever is the last person standing will be the one. Why should the champion share his prize!?"

That was when dad's men began shooting them up. Reggie and I hit the deck. There were bullets flying everywhere. One of dad's men crashed through the glass in the skylights and swung down to the floor on a rope. When he got down, he strapped a couple of harnesses on Reggie and me, and the helicopter pulled us up. As I was going up, I looked down and all the Brotherhood men were being slaughtered. They were caught - with their pants down- literally. There was one very big ugly man remaining. He had the neck of Godzilla. He was full of blood, too. He had blood on his hands, his chest, and his clothes.

He grabbed a hold of my legs with both his arms as the helicopter lifted me and the rope angrily hoisted me up. This guy must have weighed a ton. He was very rough on my joints. There was blood on his hands. I tried to squirm, wiggle, and shake him off. It didn't work. He hung on like a mad dog.

I motioned Reggie for his gun. He quickly placed the gun in my right hand. My right hand instinctually snapped it to my left hand and I began to unload round after round into his chest. I emptied the entire gun. He fell to the ground with a thud.

When it was emptied, I kept shooting. I was so angry; my fingers did their own thing. I had to tell myself that the man fell.

Reggie yelled, "the man is dead. He's dead!"

We watched them all get shot from the helicopter. There was not one person from the Brotherhood standing. I must have hit a soft spot in their egos. I didn't care. I just wanted to see the outcome of this mini war. After what seemed to be a very, very, long time, everything was silent. Dad's men gave the clear signal and we were off.

When we got in the helicopter, I told the man to let us down, we had to stick to the plan. So the helicopter dropped Reggie and me ten yards from the warehouse. I signaled that it was clear, and the men loaded up and left us.

Reggie took off his shirt and gave it to me. He ran into the warehouse and got my clothes and I put them on. I gave him a long hug. I grabbed my purse and we ran over to one of the BMWs. We got in and drove away. We drove for about an hour before we could find a descent place to rest. It was a nice restaurant. I went to the bathroom, cleaned up, and brushed my hair. I came back and sat next to Reggie. I wasn't about to leave his side until I felt better. I reached over and held his hand.

Reggie said, "You have turned out to be a very strong woman. I loved you from the start."

I lovingly replied, "I love you, too."

The waitress came over to take our order. She took our order and left.

Reggie asked me, "What would you have done if I would have been killed?"

I jokingly said, "I would have found another man."

Reggie grinned, then said, "Yes, but I haven't shown you how much I love you yet."

I quickly said, "Well! You better start!"

He planted a big, wet, sloppy kiss on me. We continued to kiss the entire time while we were waiting for the food. The minute we kissed, warm tingles shot through my body, like an electric wave. I lost total control, my limbs went weak and my toes curled inside my shoes. Pleasure beyond my control flooded my soul like a giant avalanche.

The waitress placed the food on the table. She must have been standing there for a while, because I didn't notice her. The entire restaurant was quiet. Everybody was watching us. The waitress cleared her throat several times before we realized she was standing there. When we finally looked up, the whole restaurant gave us a large handclap. I began to blush. Reggie, on the other hand, stood up and took a bow. He was not coy at all was he?

We ate the food. We were almost done eating when my cell phone rang. I picked it up and said, "The Son."

The deep, raspy voice on the other end said, "You bitch, you're not dead yet!"

I replied, "Listen here you Scumbag! I told you that I don't die easy! Now it's your turn. I'm going to hunt you down like a fucking baboon!" The minute I said that, it clicked in me how they had been tracking us. It was the phone. I abruptly got up, ran outside and smashed the phone on the pavement. Oh! Was I upset! He was just a pig! I stayed out there pacing back and forth, fuming.

Reggie paid for the food and left a five-dollar tip. He came outside, put his strong sensuous arms around me and escorted me to the Beamer.

"Reggie," I said, "We need to buy another car. I can't stand riding in this thing." He agreed. We went looking for a place to purchase a used vehicle. We found a little dealer and got a three thousand-dollar green Jeep Grand Cherokee. We traded the BMW in for it. The dealer thought he got a steal. I thought so too, since we just took the car.

We got into the Grand Cherokee and took off. I let Reggie drive. I had to call dad. I used the mini phone on my belt to phone dad.

The phone rang. Dad picked up the phone. I said, "Dad, I need your help. Mr. Zum captured Reggie and me and almost killed us. I need you to locate him because I want to execute him myself!"

Dad sternly replied, "Sonthy, you are not a killer. Let somebody else do it. Once you kill, you will always have it on your conscience."

I thought a little, then I said, "But dad! I really hate him. He just crawls on my skin. What can I do?"

Dad softly said, "Let it go. Just let it go."

"But dad! He just tried to kill me! And he murdered mom!" I could feel myself getting worked up again.

Dad said, "Will you promise to let it go? Come on, just give me your word."

I thought some more. I said, "I promise, but I'll see to it that he doesn't have a company to work for. The Brotherhood, Inc. is going down!"

Dad said, "Thank you."

I told dad, "Thanks for talking. I'll call you later."

We headed down Interstate 95 to Titusville, Florida. We were going to the John F. Kennedy Space Center. The FBI and the CIA had made arrangements for the space shuttle, Mayflower, to take us to the International Space Station. The Mayflower was one of those space shuttles that had the cargo bay turned into a bussing area with one hundred seats. The inside looked like a regular airplane. They had a large, flat television set in the front. Everybody watched the take off, as if the television screen was a window. They had little cameras outside, somewhere on the wings. The cameras filmed everything while we were in flight. I was going to the space station to talk about our plan for the war against the Brotherhood, Inc. I was also going to get a chance to work on my Sister Earth project while I was out there.

I was excited about the Sister Earth project, but I was more excited about destroying the Brotherhood, Inc. How in the world could a person clone other humans, then gut their parts out like they were animals? Everyone had a right to life, except the Zum Man or any other person who wanted to play God.

Stealing other people's organs in the name of money and power was unethical in my book. Maybe I should have learned to kill the killers! If I had not had given dad my word, I would have already been killing somebody! I did not even know why I didn't. They just pissed me off to no end! The Brotherhood, Inc. was the most disgusting company I had ever worked for.

The scheduled flight wasn't for another two weeks. Reggie and I would be in Titusville in about an hour. When we got there, we decided to rent a place for a month. We found a place on the beach. It was a house owned by one of the shuttle pilots. It was good to have connections. The beach house was very large. It was a cream color brick house. It had a sliding patio door off the kitchen, with a large white patio. The warm sea breeze made musical peace in the house.

We always left the windows open. We had two weeks to play. I didn't know how long we were supposed to stay in space at the International Space Center, so we decided to rent the beach house for a month, or maybe longer, if necessary. No Brotherhood men came after us after I smashed the phone. I had not seen any action for a day and a half. That was very good.

The only problem was that my hormones were back! I didn't even realize they were gone. Reggie sure looked good.

I called dad to let him know we were alright. He was very pleased that the drive went well. He just wondered why it took us so long to realize that it was the phone that had the locator in it. I didn't even think that the Brotherhood could be that smart.

Chapter 7
The Relationship

It was in the middle of the afternoon when we finished shopping. We got some new furniture for the house. We bought a living room set. The love seat, sofa, and chair were fluffy and soft covered with dark purple leather. We got a coffee table that had brass legs. We bought a nice, large, round, white, shaggy oriental rug and placed it under the coffee table. The place had four bedrooms, but we only furnished two of the bedrooms. We got a brass king-sized bed. We decked the bed with a large cream color comforter. We got matching sheets and king-sized pillows. We bought some oak dressers, and had some people put in beautiful curtains all over the house. The vans came to drop off everything. The interior decorators and everybody's uncle under the sun came to help us decorate the place to make it homey.

After everything was done, we decided to go swimming. The entire backyard was sandy. It led directly to the ocean. I always wanted to have a sandy beach in my backyard. I thought it was cool.

Reggie got his swimming suit on. I had a gold colored two-piece suit with black trimming. I thought it would make my figure enticing. I wanted Reggie to take a very close look at the full picture. Yes! I wanted his eyes to glide over my curves like oil. He took notice as soon as I came out into the living room! "Oh Yeah!" I was dressed to get wet all right. I intended to. Reggie's eyes widened with passionate excitement, as if a hurricane or fire had just stirred his soul. His eyes were like hawk eyes. They silently and emotionally tasted my voluptuous curves, like warm, yellow honey, shinning in the sunlight. He held himself back like a lion, waiting in the grassy plains, to violently pounce on his prey and devour the spoils hungrily, clawing, pawing, and ripping through moist tasty juices. I could almost see saliva building behind his mouth, anticipating a moist, passionate kiss.

As I walked by, he quickly stood up, ran behind me, and softly caressed my waist with his soft warm palm. My body reacted immediately. My toes dug into the carpet. I gasped for breath. My head tilted back as I stretched my neck upon his smooth shaven face. He began to gently kiss my neck and my ear lobe. I closed my eyes and gasped for air. I forgot how a kiss could arouse the beast, deep within my pelvis. Juices were flowing. I tried to ignore them. He took his left hand and slowly ran his fingers through my hair while his right hand slowly crawled around my flat belly and went to my cleavage. He caressed my breasts for the first time since we had been together. My nipples came alive. They stood to attention like they were anticipating a warm and wet mouth to tenderly love them indefinitely. His right hand slowly came over my belly button and into my bikini bottom. I felt his large hands ravish themselves through my blonde jungle and then…oooh, huh, ah, ah mmmmm, yea! His index finger and his middle finger began to quietly negotiate with my golden increment. For a minute, I couldn't handle the intense pleasure. My knees got weak and I melted into his arms. I quickly reached into my bikini bottom. I reached into my bikini with my slender fingers to pull his hand out of my utopian controller. I took off running. I ran and ran for the beach.

The warm sand spoke poetry to my feet, as I glided across it like a light and happy feather. With my arms extended in front of me, I plunged headfirst into the ocean. I swam deep down like an erectile, searching for the G-spot. Then, I came up for air just in time to see Reggie sprint to the sea across the white sand.

He ran with perfect strides. His arms swung back and forth in an L- shape. His face looked like a determined, fierce warrior. His pecks jiggled up and down. They took turns begging for more velocity. His thighs peaked with definition like slabs of marble that had veins growing over it. He extended his arms over his head and took the plunge. A clean splash hyphenated his smooth entrance into the water. He swam around me in the similitude of a dolphin. The ocean complimented his streamline body. He came up for air in front of me, tightly pressing his abdomen and chest against mine.

I felt his hard rock down below. It was pressing between my legs, desiring to open the door. But the strings bolted the door. He kissed me and I lost it. I fiercely started groping his thick hard member, as if I never had felt one before. I moved my feet back and forth like flippers to stay afloat. I wanted him inside me right now. I pulled his swimming suit down and brought it out. I tried to slide it between my bikini and my thigh, but the bikini was too tight. I wanted to do it right there in the water.

He said, "No don't! Too many people are swimming around us. Tonight when the moon is clear, we can come back." I got mad. I pushed him away and swam for shore. I got to shore, got out of the water and briskly walked into the house. I wanted his member, right then! He would not give it to me. I glanced out of the corner of my eye as I watched him. He just kept swimming, floating on his back and enjoying himself.

I came inside the house. I took a shower and then I got dressed and started making dinner. I didn't know what I was going to make, but I certainly was chopping the onions destructively! I decide to make pork chops and rice. I sauté some asparagus in white wine.

I set the table and placed two long candles on it. I turned on the stereo with some soft romantic music. I was just turning around when Reggie kissed my neck. I didn't hear him come in. I turned around and pushed his chest. Then, I said, "Hey there, mister, none of that stuff. I'm hungry."

He friskily replied, "And I thought I was your dinner. Maybe I'm your dessert?"

"Maybe," I sensually replied.

Like a gentleman, he pulled out my chair for me. I slowly and graciously sat down. I snuck a peek at him while I was sitting down. He had his huge grin again. I loved his grins. They were very sexy. He had all these bright white teeth gently outlined with perfectly defined lips. He got those devious smirks.

After I sat down, like a buck in heat, he proudly walked over to his chair that I strategically located right next to me. He sat down next to me like he used to do when we were kids. He placed his left leg over my right thigh. I lovingly smiled and started eating my food. I placed each bite into my mouth, as if I tasted his lips. I made throaty moaning noises to let him know I was still turned on.

He devoured his pork chops, like a linebacker tackling his opponent. I stared at him for about sixty seconds, then busted out laughing. I said, "Do you realize that your pork chops are already dead?"

He looked up, made a grunt and continued to ferociously engage in his eating adventure. His eating was very entertaining. I was definitely amused. If amusing me was what he was trying to do, it worked, but something else happened, too! I was definitely wet. I had to get my mind off my hormones, so I looked out the window. The sun was setting. The ocean salt was in the air. The yellow light was painting orange and yellow colors on the walls and the furniture. A yellow tint crossed his lips. I reached out with my right index finger and touched his bottom lip. They were soft and warm. There we were, the sun setting, yellow, orange and purple lights calmly kissed our love. Suddenly, we both started to stare into each other's eyes. He reached out and lifted both my hands. He quietly stood up and I stood up with him. The music began to play. I was playing a love song. He pulled me closer to him. He placed his left cheek on my left cheek and we began to dance, gently swaying back and forth. The rhythm caught us into oblivion. We were in a fantasy world, surrounded by roses. The whole planet was filled with roses.

The sweet aroma of the flowers created the clouds. The smell was coming from millions of pink, white, yellow, red, purple, and any other color of rose the imagination could conceive. We danced in the midst of the flowers as our spirits began to lift. We turned 'round and 'round as we slowly flew straight up. We entered the pink clouds. The fragrances from the Cumulus cloud seized us with overwhelming beauty and pleasure.

White doves were kindly flying around us with roses in their beaks. Some of them even stopped to chat with us while they hovered in the air like hummingbirds. They told us hidden mysteries of love. We believed every word they said.

Then the CD was done and there was nothing but silence in the house. We stared into each other's eyes some more. We didn't speak a word. We drank each other's souls like champagne or precious wine. As our eyes drank in each other's beauty, we became intoxicated with visions of pleasures. We examined each other's souls like eternal soul mates, diving so deep there was no bottom. There was a knowing, a knowing that passed all understanding, multitudes of words in pictures that had been said, but never uttered.

For the first time in my life, I saw how much this man loved me. His eyes, spirit, and soul said it all. As I gazed into his eyes, like a lighthouse shines light into the night, my heart and soul filled up with his presence. God's joy encompassed my being and I melted into everlasting oblivion. Ah! So this is what it was like to fall in love, to be out of control and lost in total trust. Lost in the ocean of love to float aimlessly without direction or haste, ah yes! To live and love is the highest trophy.

We moved our dancing into the bedroom. We danced over to the bed and glided onto the soft, white, silk sheets. We glided like feathers, gently floating to the ground. Then we laid down in harmony. I instinctively pressed the play on the stereo above my bed's headboard. As the classical music began and the moonlight gleamed through our windows and accentuated the curves of our bodies, he slowly began to undress me. The moment was very tender. Tears built up behind my eyes. I was trying not to let them pour like a cool stream flowing down the smooth hillside. They came anyway. Silent silver tears slowly caressed my cheeks.

I was dangerously happy. How could I express so many emotions? I had never had so many feelings whirling around in me like multiple hurricanes.

He unbuttoned my blouse. He carefully lifted my bra straps, one by one, off my shoulders. His hands glided up my spine and unfastened the straps. My bra and my blouse both plopped on the bed behind me. I ran my fingers through his soft, hairy chest and messaged his pectorals as I went. I began to kiss his chest. I started to reach down into his shorts. I gently lifted the heavy organ into both my hands. I began to kiss his six packs of muscles rippling his abdomen. I slid my tongue down past his belly button and onto his organ. I licked the member on all sides. He moaned with deep, throaty gasps. I placed the whole organ into my moist mouth and let it slide inside. I pulled it out softly and again, gently swallowed it. He gasped with deep sighs and breaths. His head fell backward onto the large, white, fluffy pillows.

The violins played their part in the middle of our symphony. I reached a strong note as the flutes took over. I was enjoying myself while I glided his member back and fourth in my mouth. With my left hand, I played with my Special Moment. I felt a rush of something warm filling my cheeks, without tasting it, I quickly swallowed. I felt his member twitch between my fingers. I was in total violation of my own moral dilemmas. It was sheer pleasure that burst the gates between my thighs. I had come to the edge of the mountain and rain down my fountain of youth.

Reggie pulled me up to his chest, and I laid on it and fell asleep. We slept through the night like the angels. The sunrise was the first thing to wake us and warm my cheeks. I smiled when he opened his big blue eyes. I kissed his nose and said, "I get the shower first!"

I was filled with energy, energy that was created from happiness! The kind of natural high that runners got. I was happy! I took a long graceful shower, lathering my long, blonde hair and every inch of my body that my hands could reach. I went to the bedroom after my shower. The bed was made, my clothes were neatly folded and placed on top of my pillow, and most of all, I smelled sausage and eggs throughout the house.

I got dressed and came to the kitchen table. I sat down, placed a white napkin on my shirt like a baby's bib, and picked up a knife and a fork. I began pounding on the table with the utensils grabbed tightly in my fists. I began to chant my ferocious food song, as if I was back in high school pounding on the lunchroom table along with all my friends. I sang, "Trick or treat, smell my feet, give me something good to eat." Reggie laughed as he brought breakfast and placed it on the table in front of me. We both ate our food with scrumptious smiles.

That day, we decided to rent a yacht for the entire day. We went grocery shopping and brought some food with us on the boat. We got some champagne, some grapes, some baby oil, and some condoms in case.... well.... I don't think that was going to happen. But he was so handsome. I really wanted to. I could not decide with him. See, I wanted to wait until we got married. Reggie had not said anything to me about the wedding date yet. I would try not to give him any until then, but I was not promising anything. He got me all worked up and then I wanted to eat him! I just had to find ways to keep my heart from him a little bit. I loved him so much, I thought I was going to burst! This must have been a disease! Sometimes I walked around the house thinking that one-day, maybe one day, this stuff would be all over with. We would have our little house on a lake. Maybe we would even have a log cabin with a warm and snuggly fireplace.

I thought about my children being born with little hands and fingers. I would smile at my little son and try to get him to smile back. Or maybe we would even have a girl, too, and I could braid her ponytails. We could take baths together and splash bubbles all over the bathtub. I could see myself being a good mommy. I could see two children swinging on the swings in our backyard.

I was really deep in thought. I didn't notice Reggie standing behind me with his arm around my waist until he said, "Penny for your thoughts." I told him they were worth a nickel. He smiled and said, "How about you tell me some of these thoughts on the yacht."

We drove over to the marina. We met the captain. His name was Fred. He was a sweet old man in his seventies. He looked like Santa Claus. He had a short beard and a black tux. Classical music was playing when we got on the boat. Fred was a wise man. I signaled to Reggie, and Reggie said to Fred, "Take her out!"

The boat pulled out slowly and turned towards the sunrise. It was about five-thirty in the morning. We wanted to have a long, easy day. We walked up to the bow in front of the boat. First, Reggie laid down on his back on one of the plush seats. I glided my body on top of his. I turned to my right side, against the wall. I snuggled under his armpit. When I was nice and comfortable, I laid my head on his chest. But I wasn't completely comfortable yet until I had stretched my left arm over his chest. I rested my palm on his right pectoral. I watched his chest slowly rise up and down as I listened to his strong heartbeat. We lay there for about five minutes without saying a word.

Reggie reached into his white shorts pocket and pulled out a quarter. He placed it on top of my hand. I glanced over at it. Then I pondered my first thought. After, a while I said, "When do you want to get married?"

He said, "I was thinking this summer. What do you think?"

I thought for a minute. Actually, I was delighted. It didn't matter when. I was just eager to get married. There was so much excitement bottled up in me about it. I said, "Let me call my Dad and let him know that we will be married this summer."

He said, "Do you want to talk about it first?"

I told him, "I'll talk about it when I get back. I have to call Dad." So I got up, went back in the boat, got the phone and came out. I laid back in the same position and with my left thumb I pressed the redial button.

Dad answered the phone. "What is it, Sonthy?"

"Well, I have good news. We are going to get married on my birthday this summer on June fifteenth."

Dad excitedly replied, "Well that's great news! I'm happy for you. I'll set it on the calendar and my people will have everything ready when you get down here."

"Thanks, Dad. I love you very much. Bye, bye," He said bye and hung up the phone. When I got off the phone. I said, "Reggie, Dad want's us to have it down there. Do you mind?"

Reggie excitedly replied, "Of course not! That will be splendid!"

Then I said, "Now what is it that you wanted to talk about?"

He said, "I was going to ask you which date we should pick, but you beat me to the punch. June fifteenth will be perfect, I never forget your birthday, so I won't forget the anniversary."

He continued, "I have to tell you something else. Do you remember my Ma and Pa?"

"Yeah, what about them?" I said.

He sadly said, "My Dad was shot and killed by the Zum Man, too. I took Mom and hid her. I send her money so she can live. I want to send her to Norbert. Would that be okay with you? She has been living in isolation for two years now." Little tears started to roll down my strong man's cheeks. He continued, "I want her to give me away. You knew that I was the only child right?"

"Yea," I said.

"I want to call her on your phone and then I'll call Norbert and tell him I want her to live with him. I'm a little afraid for her. They are pretty resourceful. They might find her." I quickly handed him the phone and sat up.

He dialed the phone. It rang. A lady answered it. She said, "Hello. Is it you, Reggie?"

"Yea ma it's me. Sonthy and I picked next summer on June fifteenth to get married. I want you to give me away. Would that be okay? Ma, remember our discussion about living with Norbert? Well, Sonthy says that it's okay. So you better start packing." She was very excited, I could hear her voice loudly on the other end.

She said, "I would love to. When do I get to meet Sonthy? I haven't seen her for so long?"

Reggie quickly handed me the phone and said, "Mom wants to know when she will be able to see you. Why don't you tell her yourself? Anytime is fine with me."

I grabbed the phone and put it to my ear. I was pretty excited to talk to her. I said, "Hello, Mrs. Wheaties?"

"Hi, Sonthy. My, your voice sounds so grown up! I hear you have the date set?"

I eagerly replied, "We certainly did! I want to see you. Reggie said anytime would be good for him. What about you?"

She replied, "Anytime is good."

"How about we come over tomorrow, stay for a week or until everything's packed and moved out?"

She replied, "That would be fine."

I said, "I'll see you tomorrow!" I handed the phone back to Reggie.

He said, "Tell Aunt Josey and Uncle Paul that we'll land a double-bladed helicopter on their farm about one o'clock tomorrow morning. We'll help you load the stuff and we'll be off. Bye, Ma," she hung up.

Reggie gave me the phone. I called dad again. "What is it, Sonthy? Are you alright?"

I replied, "Yea, Dad, I'm okay. Reggie wants his Ma to live down there with you guys. She is not too safe where she is. The Zum Man killed Mr. Wheaties. Would that be okay?"

"That would be most splendid. We have a lot of catching up to do." Dad eagerly said.

I continued, "Dad can you send a double-bladed helicopter to pick us up at ten o'clock tonight. We have to be their tomorrow morning at one. We rented a yacht. We are on it right now. I still have my belt on. You just call me when they are in our area and we will set off some flares. Bye, Dad." He agreed and said, "Goodbye." I hung up the phone.

When I hung up the phone, I looked at Reggie and he was wearing his content grin. I said, "Hey there, young man, what's that grin all about?"

Reggie replied, "I'm glad she got a chance to talk to you. She has been asking for you for a number of years now. Finally, she's going to meet you."

I kissed him gently on his lips. He responded by running his fingers through my hair. He said, "You know, I have loved you so long. For you to be lying in my arms is a dream come true. Remember how we use to pray? Remember we took the oath under prayer that we would love each other forever?"

My mind quickly flashed back to that time. It was winter when he came over that Saturday morning. We had just finished eating breakfast and I was doing dishes. Reggie just walked in the house, pulled up a chair next to mine and started helping me wash the dishes. That's when he gave me my first kiss. We had just finished washing and drying the dishes. We were getting down off our chairs. He got down first and then, like a polite little gentleman he was, he helped me down. I placed both my hands on his shoulders and he placed his hands on my waist. He held onto me when I landed. That's when our eyes first met. We stared at each other for a long time. Then he placed both his little palms on my cheeks and kissed me. I quickly push his chest and he fell on the chair and sat down. I came over and sat on his lap and put my arms around him. Then I said, "Do you promise not to ever leave me? Do you promise to love me forever like Mommy loves Daddy? Huh! Cute punk?"

He replied, "Yup! Forever and ever and ever!" He was so cute. He bobbed his head up and down when he was saying, "ever and ever." Then we held hands, put the chairs side by side and knelt in front of them. That's when we prayed.

I prayed first. I said, "Jesus can you come into our hearts and keep us together forever? He's my Cute Punk."

Reggie prayed. "Jesus if we ever separate, my Daddy told me that you can bring us back together again. Please, will you do that?"

Then I jumped in and said, "Yeah! You're supposed to do that you know, 'cause you are God. You're suppose to do everything!" Then we said our Amen and thank you.

Reggie was reminding me of that prayer. I said, "Hey. I never said I would love you forever. I said for him to keep us together forever."

He quickly replied, "That's the same. Why would you want to be with me forever if you didn't love me? I told you back then that I would marry you. I told you that you loved me, but you didn't know it yet."

I said, "I don't remember all of that." But I remembered all of that all right. I couldn't get him out of my heart. But I definitely tried. I tried with Charles. But it didn't work, even though the sex was great!

Then he sat up and said, "What! You don't remember that?"

I started to laugh, then I said, "Nope! Not a thing!"

Then he started singing, "Liar, liar, pants on fire! Your nose is long as a telephone wire!" I tackled him and we started to wrestle on the bow of the yacht.

I said, "I can still whip your butt."

He replied, "Go ahead! You're just going to love me more after I start to crying! You always did and you always will!" I laid on top of him and looked into his eyes. I gave him a powerful deep and moist kiss. He kissed back and started fondling my butt.

I loved it when he touched my butt. It was like electrical sensations shot up and down my spine when he touched me. We rolled around the bow for a little bit. Then he stood up and escorted me to the chamber bedroom. We quickly undressed and went in the shower. He turned on the shower and cold water sprayed on me. I let out a sharp "yelp!" like a puppy. Then I hugged him. I felt his heavy organ touching my pubic area. Suddenly my body woke up. My nipples got hard and I felt a pulsating urge building up in my utopian treasure. He kissed me like a passionate lover from the 17th century. He grabbed my butt and my upper thigh and lifted me up onto his pelvis. His heavy member was eagerly searching for the doorway to heaven! It kept ringing the doorbell. Indeed the doorbell was lit up. My body slipped over his because of the lathering soap. My breasts delighted in all the affection and attention they were receiving. The warm water continued to pour on us gently. Then Reggie's mouth began the journey. He kissed my neck, then my breast entered into his warm moist mouth. I was lost. He drove me into total insanity. His lips and tongue opened the door to heaven! His tongue entered the opening and I almost fainted. He sucked on my lollipop and licked inside me with fervency. I felt lightheaded and out of control. I held onto his head with both my claws. Like a cat squeezing a pigeon's life! Oh, humm, yea! Mmun. Please, please, I beg you Reggie! Please. My thighs started to quiver. Oh my God! What's happening? I had never felt like this. It made me afraid. I pushed him away, ran out of the shower and grabbed a towel. I quickly dried off. Reggie just stayed in the shower and finished his bathing. I quickly got dressed and sat on the bed with my legs folded Indian style. I waited for him to come out. When he came out he got dressed. It was time for lunch. Wow! It was two o'clock in the afternoon already. We called for the cook.

The cook made us some nice food. It was nothing too exciting. We decided that after lunch we were going to just sit on the bow and talk. We went upstairs on the bow. We sat on a couple of white chairs that were out there. The yacht was rather large. We could have been on one end of it and never had to see anybody for hours. Our thing was being out in the open air. The inside was pretty, but the open air was prettier. The wind was blowing my hair as I stood there, holding onto the front railing. I could smell the salty spray of ocean mist as the yacht bounced over the waves. The ocean was deep blue. I remembered the second time I went out on it. It was the time my dad got his leg eaten by that stupid killer whale.

I was thinking about that when Reggie came up next to me and just stood there and looked at the vast blue wonder. We both stood there for about an hour without saying a word to each other. One of the reasons I loved Reggie was because I didn't always have to talk to him. He knew when to just leave me alone. It was like he was connected to me by some invisible cord. He just let me be. I never felt that I needed time from him, because he gave me lots of time. It was like he heard my heart beat and just flowed with it.

He gently rubbed my back and said, "You know, when they killed Dad, I refused to sleep with their genetic women. I went ballistic on them. They had to chase me for months. I was on a rampage, destroying every Brotherhood thing I could lay my hands on. They caught me and tied me up and beat me until I ended up in the hospital. I had a cracked rib for a long time. I decided, while I was in the hospital, that I would play along until one day I got my opportunity. But I tried, like hell, to get away."

My heart broke in two when I heard that. I turned around and hugged him. When the hugging was done, he continued, "Then, I numbed my heart and started sleeping with whomever they wanted. I would work all day and at night, they would send me out on appointments. I was so glad you came along. I was losing my soul. I was sliding into this deep, dark abyss. It was engulfing me. I didn't know right from wrong anymore, until I watched you for a while. You brought me hope. You give me a desire to live and love."

I started crying. I didn't know why I started crying. Tears just bubbled up inside of me. Then they gushed out like a water fountain. I softly began to caress his face. I said in a deeper tone, "I'm here honey. We will destroy that Corporation. That's a promise!"

He smiled, wiped my tears with his T-shirt, and put his arm around me. We stared into the deep for another forty-five minutes. I turned to him and said, "Reggie, my greatest fear was that I would never love. I would be an old lady, doing research. I would be lonely and God-forsaken for the rest of my life. I didn't know that love could fill a person so much. It makes you just want to yell Hallelujah! I hate being alone. I need someone to listen to me. Someone that I know is taking me seriously. I need someone who will respond to me, and not to my behavior. You always have done that Reggie. I thought I would never see you again. I wish I could say you are my life Reggie, but I know you better. You are a stinker!" We both laughed. It felt so good to laugh. It was healing. Something inside of me was melted away like scales plucked off a fish.

Speaking of fish, I was hungry again. The sun was going down. We spent all day talking. I poured out my heart to Reggie, like milk rushing from a milk stream, white and smooth coming down the side of a mountain. My heart was like a mountain. An unclimbable peak, but Reggie scaled it with ease. He opened his heart for me for the first time since I could remember. We did so much talking that I heard his words for days going around in my head.

We came inside and ate dinner. We snuggled and watched satellite television until we heard the helicopter outside. They didn't need the flares. They saw the boat's lights. The double-bladed thing hovered over the boat like some monster. Wind currents blew violently from the blades. First, I climbed up into it. Reggie followed. The boat turned around and headed back for shore.

I was surprised. As I got in the helicopter, dad was there. I screamed, "Dad! Oh Dad!" I hugged him for a long time. I introduced Reggie, "Dad, this is Reggie. Reggie remember Dad?"

They both shook hands and at the same time they both said, "Hi!"

Dad said, "It's good to see you children are safe and sound. I came along, even though it was dangerous because I wanted to see you and your mother together. Besides, I missed my Sonthy! So Reggie, can you go over and sit next to that pilot and help him get to where he is going. I've read your file and you know how to drive almost anything. Very impressive, Son."

Reggie had that grin again. Then he said, "Thanks, I work at it." Reggie scooted into the pilot's seat and off we went.

Dad and I got reacquainted on our ride to Reggie's aunt's house. There were two more helicopters behind us, and a couple of fighters escorting them. That made me feel real safe. I had not felt that safe for a very long time.

We arrived at Reggie's aunt's house. All the airplanes and the helicopters landed, but the fighters hovered. The men quickly and systematically moved Mrs. Wheaties' stuff into the second helicopter. It took a half an hour. Then we were off. The fighters and the helicopters flew for a number of uncountable hours. I wasn't really paying attention. I was busy listening to Mrs. Wheaties stories. The vehicles landed in the middle of nowhere once, to refuel, and then we were off again. I figured we were heading to the Island of Patmos.

The ride was rather smooth. The airships landed at Patmos International Airport. There was a limousine there to pick us up. The security men quickly escorted us to the king's limousine. We piled in and off we went. The driver took us to this huge, white palace. I figured it was dad's house. The limousine pulled up under the carport in the back of the mansion. There were people all over the place ready to greet us. This was kind of exciting! The King! Mmmm, he's just Norbert. What the hell was all this fuss about? I just played along.

The next morning, during breakfast, dad needed to talk. He said, "Plans have changed. We have to take the space shuttle that is leaving today. After breakfast, the limousine will take us to the airport. From there, we will take seven fighters to the Kennedy Space Center. All three of us will be riding in separate airplanes. Each of us will ride right behind the pilot. Make sure you do not touch anything while you are back there. My plane will lead the way. Yours and Reggie's will be side by side. We will have two fighters escorting my plane and two will be escorting both of yours. Sonthy, your escort will be on your right, and Reggie's escort will be on his left. At the International Space Station the FBI and CIA will brief us on the strategies we will be using. It was time for war."

Chapter 8

Walking the Light

"The Royal Wedding with Izizi Vuvu"

The meeting in space wasn't anything I had expected. But I can't talk about that right now. On our way back in the space shuttle, Reggie, dad, and I talked about the wedding. I told dad that the wedding date was coming up soon, and here we were talking about war! We should be talking about my wedding. Dad agreed that we should be talking about the wedding, so he decided that the minute we got back to the palace, he was going to hire the world famous wedding consultant Izizi Vuvu. I agreed to have Izizi Vuvu be our wedding consultant. Mr. Vuvu specialized in royal weddings. Dad agreed to pay for everything except the rings. I wasn't expecting him to get them, anyway. Reggie and I were going to go shopping together and buy them. Buying rings was the first thing on our agenda.

Being on earth again felt very strange. I felt so heavy. I'm sure I didn't gain weight out in space. I knew this because we ate gook out there. I was glad to walk on solid ground again.

The shuttle landed on schedule. We ran through the checks and three days later, they let us go. The same airplanes we took to the Kennedy Space Center were the same ones that brought us back. When we finally landed at Patmos, I was exhausted. Reggie on the other hand wanted to play. I didn't know how he could get two hours of sleep every night and still function as well as he did.

As soon as we got in the palace, dad went to bed. I took a nap, too. Reggie went for a walk on the beach. After I woke up, dad had dinner ready. We all ate like pigs. Let me guess why we ate so much food, mmm could it be that we ate gook for the past month, nah! Reggie and I went to bed right away after dinner.

The next day, Reggie and I decided to go shopping. Dad made this big fuss about bodyguards. I told him we could take care of ourselves, but he didn't want any argument, so I went with the flow. We had to lug ten bodyguards around all day. For Pete's sake! They even watched us when we bought the rings and had a moment of romance in the jewelry store. These men needed to get a life. None of them broke out into smiles when we kissed during the trial placing of the wedding bands. They kept faces that looked like those short, flat-faced dogs, ah, what do you called them....oh, yea, Boxers. The only people that clapped and smiled for us were the customers and sales people in the store. They liked how Reggie made a spectacle of himself.

He got on both his knees, looked up at me, and held out the ring, and said, "Will you marry me?" I could see behind his eyes, those happy, silent tears. I had never seen Reggie cry since he had been grown up. No tears actually came out, but I could tell.

It was so moving I just gushed out and eagerly said, "Yes! Yes! You know that I want to marry you!" The whole place started clapping and cheering, except for the Boxers.

On our way back from the mall, I used the limousine's phone and called Izizi Vuvu. I told him I wanted a meeting right away. We needed to discuss the things I wanted in the wedding. Mr. Vuvu promptly agreed. I thought, he had better agreed. Dad was paying him a million and a half to put on a good show!

Reggie sat tentatively with me while I discussed every detail with Izizi. I told Izizi that he needed to be completely conscious to follow the proper royal guidelines. I didn't want to embarrass my father. I told him that I wanted the streets, churches, and the palace decorated. I told him that he was in charge of the engagement party too. I only wanted close family, friends, and some of dad's foreign dignitaries to be invited to the party. Izizi agreed on everything.

He said, in a strange French accent, "Mademoiselle, I understand how important this wedding is to you. I shall place grace and class in your wedding. Even you will be surprised. You will say, 'Bravo, Izizi Vuvu!'"

Mr. Vuvu only had two months to make this wedding happen. It was already Monday and Mr. Vuvu had turned dad's palace into a zoo. His employees were running to and fro. Dad had a special room set up for Mr. Vuvu's office. He was there day and night. This guy was as bad as Reggie, he never slept. People were coming and going. Things were being set up. What a mad house!

Saturday was going to be the engagement party. Things were moving fast. Mr. Vuvu didn't waste any time. Reggie was very amused by Mr. Vuvu and his people. He thought they were elegant. They had great pride in their work. Women were singing as they worked, men were cracking jokes I had never heard, and music was all over the palace.

Reggie said, "Does Mr. Vuvu know that the wedding is June fifteenth?"

"I told him ten times."

Mr. Vuvu was a genius. He conducted everything with perfect symphony. He had the whole palace decorated in purple and ivory. He even had fancy gold and purple streamers going up the ivory steps to the double-sided, circular balcony.

As you entered the large, gold, double doors of the palace-the type of doors that stood about fifteen feet high- you come into a very large majestic opening. It had a dome in the ceiling that let golden sun shine reflect off the chandelier and gloriously illuminated the room. About a hundred feet straight ahead was the wide, marble staircase. The white, marble floor led to the white staircase. At the top of the stairs, there was a circular, indoor balcony that went completely around the room.

Reggie wasn't acting his usual self that day.

I said, "Honey, are you alright?"

"I have a mild headache and I feel a little warm. We did too much running around today. I'm a little tired."

Reggie tired! Hah! That would be the day. He was like plutonium; he never ran low on energy. I noted it, but Reggie told me it was nothing. He told me that every once and a while he just got a little frustrated, and it probably showed.

Saturday was here! Wee! Reggie and I slept real sound that night. I loved the smell of the man. It was like musk. You know the kind that got your pheromones all worked up! I felt like pouncing on him like a wild beast in the night, crawling through the grass and leaping upon my helpless victim, ferociously untamed. My underground river of wine was flowing. Like juices from the grapevine that had fermented for a hundred years. I was waiting to be tasted, ah! I wanted him now! Gimme, yum, yum!

Suddenly, I heard my mother's voice, say, "Sonthy!" I looked around, thinking maybe she was really there, but she wasn't. She was gone forever.

I kissed Reggie and sat up in bed. He slowly opened his eyes and smiled. Then he said, "Morning."

I replied, "Morning to you too, Snug Bug."

He got out from under the sheets and laid his strong, warm chest on my naked back and gently caressed my breast. The minute he touched my breast, lightening shot through me like a thousand bolts of wild electricity! I leaned my head back into his shoulders and moaned like a yelping puppy. Reggie quickly placed his right hand over my mouth. Then he bent over and started to whisper.

"I had this dream that you were a wild cheetah, crawling through grass. You found a young male buck with three points and quietly unleashed all your animal energy on the deer. As you landed with all your might, the deer turned into a river of sweet, red wine. I was on the bank of the river, drinking the wine with my entire face buried in the flow. That's when I woke up as you kissed me. I think something else woke up like a dragon breathing fire."

I was too into it. I told Reggie, "Wait a minute. Just wait. It's too close to the wedding. I want to save it for the honeymoon. You know that." Reggie's face saddened for about two seconds. He leaned me back and cupped my right breast in his big hands and began to suck. Mmm, his mouth felt so warm. I felt my heart racing again. Pleasure was screaming inside me. I couldn't take it! I pushed Reggie off me and ran to the shower.

Reggie walked into the shower in the middle of my shower. Oh, he was too gorgeous! He had those deep blue eyes, that black hair and that chiseled body. His stomach was like six cubes of bricks, placed neatly in two rows. I wanted him so bad!

I quickly got out of the shower. We both got dressed and went out to meet dad at the breakfast table. The table was outside facing the sunrise. Dad was eating breakfast with Mr.Vuvu. We both sat down next to each other. Dad was straight across from us and Mr.Vuvu was to our left.

Mr. Vuvu didn't say a word. He just plopped a large book of invitation choices in front of us and, one by one, he turned the pages. As he turned the pages, Reggie shook his head. Then the next page, and Reggie shook his head again. Well this went on for about a half-hour. He came to this page that had ivory colored invitations with gold lettering and purple wild Hyacinths on the sides. Reggie and I nodded "yes" at the same time, then we looked at each other as if to say, "Hey! Good taste."

Mr. Izizi Vuvu asked all his questions and reminded us that the party was that night. The guests would start arriving at noon for the forte entertainment. He spoke his elegant grace and paid his homage, then left.

When it was dad's turn, he said, "Let me get this right, you want Charles to be your maid of honor? and Reggie's mother to be his best man?"

I quickly replied, "Yup!" Dad rejected this thought.

He said, "I can't picture Charles as a maid of honor. He's black. I'm kind of fond of Charles, but...."

Dad just started in on me, pushing my buttons. I slammed both my hands on the table and stood up, then said in an aggressive tone, "I don't care if you are the king or God. I will have whomever I will have as my maid of honor, white, black, red, or green. Is that understood!"

The guards heard all the commotion and ran out to the porch to see what was going on. Dad raised the palm of his hand to stop them. He flicked his wrist and they were gone.

Dad looked at me and he knew he had hurt my feelings. He got up and quietly walked over to me. I was still fuming. Then he embraced me with a big hug. Reggie didn't move. He just kept on eating. This was dad's way of saying he was sorry. I forgave him. Then he sat down again.

He said, "Well, Honey, I don't agree with you, but this is your wedding, and I'm with you in any decision you make." I thanked him and gave him another hug.

Then I said, "Hey, at least I'm wearing Mom's dress, you gotta give me some credit here." Dad just smiled.

The bell lady was ringing the bell, notifying us that the guests were arriving. The music was playing, I loved the sound of that harp. It flowed like my affections for Reggie. Reggie and I held hands as we walked with dad into the royal palace.

The guards brought an incredibly large, golden chair. It had carvings and jewels all over it. I had never seen a chair so majestic. They took dad's morning coverings and put on him a black suit. On the suit there was a ten-inch wide sash, encrusted with glittering diamonds. The diamond sash went from his left shoulder down to his waist. They gave him some white gloves, and he sat down facing the double doors. One of the royal guards positioned me on dad's right side while Reggie and his mom stood next to each other on dad's left side. Finally, when everybody was in place, the royal guards stood behind us. There was another chair brought that was silver and gold. It was placed on my right side.

I heard commotion outside. The trumpets sounded, The big double doors opened and the announcer proclaimed the entrance of the Queen of England, Queen Elizabeth the II. Wow! I thought, Now that's a Queen! When I saw her, I just stared at her with my mouth opened. I was thinking, the Queen of England at my engagement party?

Dad stood up as she gracefully strolled towards us. She gave her greetings and took her chair next to me. Her royal guards stood behind her, next to dad's royal guards.

Next, through those huge doors, came some dignitaries I had never met. Some of the islanders were also invited. We already had about three hundred people in the palace, and people were still arriving. It looked like that was going to be the trend all day. We had to just stand there. Everybody that came greeted the Queen and us. Finally, an announcement was made. I thought I recognized the name. I started to move my head side to side trying to see who it was they had announced. It was hard to see through the people, until that particular person they announced started walking towards us, and then people moved over to the side and a pathway was made for the arrival.

It was Charles, I took off running towards him to hug him. A fourth of the way down the isle, one of the guards stopped me. He motioned for me to return back to my place. I turned around and looked at dad. Dad put up his right palm and motioned for me to return. One of the other guards stopped Charles at the door. I stood there for a minute, looking back and forth from Charles to dad. I was so excited that I lost the idea that I was actually a princess which I never followed much anyway. I felt the guard's hand nudge me towards my father. I blinked a couple of times, waiting for my brain to catch up and my emotions to subside. When I finally thought things through, I returned to my original position, being escorted by the royal guard.

When I finally positioned myself, the guard at the door let Charles go. He walked over to me and wanted to greet me first. I shook my head and pointed to the king. He greeted dad. They chit-chatted about them going to see some movies while he was here. He came to me. I was very excited. I had an impulse to hug him, but I had better not. So, I didn't hug him. I followed all the greeting procedures and let him do his thing. We talked a little, but he had to move on. Next, he went to Queen Elizabeth. He did his formal greeting thing and chatted with her a little about the time dad fell in the water. He told the Queen that he liked dad's artificial limb. He quickly greeted Reggie's mother, Joyce. Finally, he greeted Reggie. Reggie was very pleasant to Charles. When Charles finished his greetings, a few more people came in and greeted us. The doors were shut. It took two hours to greet everybody. It was about two o'clock.

Once everybody was settled, two trumpet blowers blew their trumpets. After the trumpets sounded, the entire room was quiet. King Savitri stood up and said a few words.

Dad said, "On behalf of my kingdom, my people, Queen Elizabeth, and my family, I welcome you to my home. We have come together to celebrate the wedding engagement of my only daughter, Dr. Sonthy Savitry to Reggie Wheat. Before my daughter can marry Reggie, he must be a prince, therefore Queen Elizabeth has joined me in witness to this bestowment. Reggie come forward and kneel."

Reggie came in front of dad and knelt. Queen Elizabeth stood up and walked over to Reggie. Dad walked over to Reggie. One of the knights brought over a purple little pillow with a tiny glass of oil on it. With both hands the Knight presented the oil. The trumpets blew again. Dad took the oil, opened it, placed his right index finger on the top of the bottle, and anointed Reggie's forehead.

Dad placed both his palms on Reggie's head and said, "With the power that has been invested in me from God, and the people of the Island of Patmos as the supreme ruler and king, I now bestow upon you the majesty of a prince. From this day forward, you and your immediate family are royalty. I bring before me this day, Queen Elizabeth the II unto a witness to thee. Blessed be thou amongst men, Prince Reggie Wheat."

When dad paused, the trumpets blew again. Dad took the petite vase of oil and gave it to Queen Elizabeth.

The Queen poured it on Reggie's head and said, "I anoint thee from on high in the name of the Father, the Son, and the Holy Ghost, to walk upright before God and man in royal majesty. This day I, Queen Elizabeth the II, witness the birth of royalty in the Wheat family by King Norbert Savitry. Go, thou, and live long, prosper, and conduct thyself wisely among men."

Dad and the Queen went back to their seats. When they sat down, the trumpets blew again. Then Reggie motioned to me to come forward. I came beside Reggie, and we both faced dad. When we came in front of dad, I turned and faced west, while Reggie turned and faced east. Reggie got on his right knee, dad took his right hand and my right hand and gave my hand to Reggie and Reggie's right hand to me.

Dad said, "I now give my daughter's hand to thee in marriage. Honor her, respect her, and most of all, love her."

We stood there, staring deep into each other's eyes, for a few minutes. Tears were slowly caressing my cheeks. Dad put up his right hand and a royal guard placed a purple little box in his hand. Dad opened the box and handed the box with the engagement ring to Reggie. Reggie took the ring and placed it on my wedding finger and said, "Your Royal Highness, will you marry me?"

"Yes, I will, your Royal Highness!"

The moment I said, "I will," everybody in the palace broke out in a standing ovation. That went on for about ten minutes. When the clapping was done, dad clapped his hand twice and the festivities and music began. Everybody was dancing and having a great time. First, dad danced with me, while Reggie danced with the queen. Next, dad danced with the queen, and Reggie danced with his mother, and I danced with Charles. Finally, Reggie danced with me, and Charles danced with Reggie's mother.

When I was dancing with Charles, I asked him why his fiancé didn't come. He said, "Vanessa, got in a car accident six months ago and passed away."

"Why didn't you e-mail me to tell me?"

He sadly replied, "I was really hurting and I needed time to myself."

I went silent.

"I'm sorry, Charles."

"No need to be sorry. I'm doing much better now, Sonthy."

We changed topics and finally started to have a good time. The party was awesome. It was the most fun, I had had in years. There was food, music, laughter, funny people, and most of all special dancers. Those dancers were my favorite.

The party was over about two o'clock in the morning. Dad, the queen, Reggie, Reggie's mom, and I had to sit down again and have everybody say their good-byes. By the time Reggie and I went to bed, it was about three thirty in the morning.

Charles stayed for about a week and then returned for my wedding. Dad and I got to do things with him. But Reggie kept his distance. All in all, I was happy.

The Wedding Day

The wedding day was finally here! I was so excited that I woke up at five o'clock in the morning. I had been anticipating that day for a long time. The streets of Patmos were decorated with American flags and Island of Patmos flags. Every street lamp or pole had flags on them. Dad made one of his speeches, and motivated the country to decorate the island. There were two flags, flying side by side, all over the streets. For the past month and a half, since the engagement party, the citizens had been decorating anything and everything.

I was very proud of Mr. Vuvu. He had the church and the palace decorated precisely the way I wanted, and then some. I couldn't brag enough about Mr. Vuvu. He conducted the entire management of the wedding explicitly well. Everybody knew exactly where they were supposed to be and what they were supposed to do. The past month had been very wearisome, but I forgot about all the rehearsals, line ups, and chaos! Things were going smooth now. Cross your fingers, and let's hope things go the way we planned.

Reggie was a little more excited than usual. He kept pacing around the palace. Mr. Vuvu assigned him somebody to help keep him on track.

The church was decorated with large vases of ivory roses and purple wild Hyacinths. At the end of the pews were little nosegays with ivory roses and purple wild Hyacinths tied by purple satin ribbons. There were special red carpets brought into the church for my procession.

All those dignitaries and regular people we invited showed up. I kept watching the news, not one person said no to my wedding. I was utterly amazed. George W. Bush, Jr. arrived on Airforce One. I never thought the President of the United States would show up to my wedding! Of course Queen Elizabeth the II showed up. I was surprised to see Queen Anne-Marie of Greece, the Crown Prince of Norway, Prince Joachim, and Princess Alexander of Denmark. I could have used a few lessons in royalty about now. On the other hand, maybe I would get too snobby. I was really excited about Prince Guillman and Princess Sibilla of Luxembourg because dad told me so much about them. Prince George of Hanover came, too. Now, he's one with personality. Dad told me a little about the Prince of Astorias but he's still a mystery to me.

Many of these people arrived in the morning. Our airport was very busy, not to mention the news media, trying to manipulate around the thousands of people in the streets who wanted to take a peak at more royalties.

I just heard the cannons go off to announce the beginning of the wedding festivities. I looked at my watch. It was 9 o'clock in the morning. They were right on schedule. The service was at one o'clock in the afternoon. They were going to parade me through the country and, hopefully, I could get to the church on time. The Royal Cortege was almost ready to leave the palace. The Patmos Chief of Police, Commander Rimkus turned on his siren and lights. First to follow Commander Rimkus, was Reggie and his mother's limousine. The second limousine was Charles and Queen Elizabeth, followed by President George Bush, Jr. All the other dignitaries' limousines followed each other in a winding parade from the palace to the church. It was now eleven thirty in the morning and dad and I had not gotten into the carriage yet! I was getting very nervous. Mr. Vuvu was suppose to call us when the first limousine arrived at the church. That was our cue to get into the carriage.

I could not believe there were so many people in the streets, on the houses, garages, and buildings. They were all over the lawns and side walks like sand. I had no clue that my love for Reggie was going to start such a mess.

Dad came running into my room. He was on the phone with Mr. Vuvu.

"Ok, Dear, it is time to go."

We had twelve Clydesdales pulling our carriage. We had tight security on every side. It was a bright, cloudless day. The sky was rich blue and I had not a worry in the world. All I could feel was the smell of roses all over the streets. The entire population of the island must have bought all the roses in the world! It was a tradition that when the king's daughter or son married, the whole nation bought at least one rose to offer the princess and prince. The minute I walked outside, I saw white roses, pink roses, yellow roses, red roses, blue roses, and purple roses. There were people holding roses in their hands, and children waving roses back and forth. I had a swelling deep inside my spirit. It was a swelling of acceptance, of love and belonging. It was something so strong, all I could do was barely hold back my tears and hold up the bouquet of roses I was carrying with me. The feeling was totally overwhelming. With six mounted royal guards leading the way in front of the Clydesdales, the golden royal carriage slowly moved through the streets of Patmos. Every time the carriage passed by a new group of people, they began singing the national anthem.

We finally got to the church at twelve forty-five in the afternoon. When we pulled up to the church, the phone rang and dad answered it. It was Izizi. He told us everything was good to go inside. Everybody was seated and the Pastor was in his place. He told dad that Reggie and his mother were now being escorted to the front of the church. He wanted us to wait about five minutes and then come in.

The people outside of the church were singing and applauding as dad and I stood up to await the royal guards to finish lying down the red carpet from the carriage to the Church. It took about five minutes.

Four trumpeters positioned themselves at the beginning of the carpet, where the carriage door was. Two trumpeters were on one side of the carpet while another two were on the other side, facing each other. Next to the trumpeters, there were little children along the side of the carpet, dressed in white holding flowers. They had them in line facing each other across the carpet. Each line began with a boy and alternated with a girl, all the way up to the church's entrance. A royal guard opened the carriage door and the trumpeters sounded, signifying that we were walking on the red carpet. They kept playing until we entered the church.

When we came inside, dad and Charles helped me arrange my dress and put the Tiara on my head and placed the veil over my face. The Tiara has been a family heirloom for generations and the veil is fifteen feet long. The netting of the veil is covered with random pearls that match the dress. I was wearing my mother's ivory silk dress. I thought it was the most beautiful dress in the world! I had to get it tailored a little. Mom had a bigger bust than I did. Mom's dress was an empire-style gown with a scooped neckline and Juliette sleeves. The bodice of the gown was lace-covered with a chapel length train covered with lace flower appliqués. The lace appliqués covered the skirt of the gown. I bought a matching pearl necklace and earrings. I even had special ivory satin dancing shoes made for me. I was planning on cutting the night with style! Mr.Vuvu handed me my Juliet bridle bouquet with ivory roses and a few purple wild hyacinths.

Dad was wearing his black formal evening tuxedo with his black full dress coat. He had on a white pique shirt under his posh tux. Dad also had on a white waistcoat, bow tie, studs, and cuff links. I liked his boutonniere. It was an ivory rosebud. Of course he had those favorite snazzy black shoes he had been polishing for years.

Reggie and Charles' tuxedos were an oxford black cutaway with an ivory double-breasted vest. They had on that smooth, sleek, charcoal gray trousers which made them look absolutely handsome. Each of them had on an ivory colored ascot with purple stripes and winged collars. Dad talked them into wearing the same type of shoes dad bought twenty-nine years ago. They had on brand new black Norbert shoes. Their pearl stick pins, with those gold cuff links and ivory colored rosebud boutonnieres, made those two gentlemen absolutely ravishing.

Joyce was sculptured into a purple, silk empire-style full-length gown with a scooped neckline. She wore a pearl necklace with matching earrings. The beautiful mother of the morning dove carried a bouquet with wild Hyacinths and a few ivory roses. Scattered among the roses were purple, satin ribbons, streaming down from the bouquet. She pranced about vitally with her one-inch satin shoes, as if she was the life of the party.

It was about ten minutes after one o'clock in the afternoon. Dad and I were ready for the presentation. Mr. Vuvu came running over to dad. He was wearing one of those cordless headphone sets. He said to dad in his French, lighthearted voice, "Your Highness, Charles will walk down the aisle and Joyce. He will escort her up the stairs to the front of the church. You and the princess will walk down the aisle to the song of *Jesu Joy of Mans Desiring*. Your Highness, upon reaching the front, you will hand your daughter's hand over to Reggie. Okay, Mr. Zimbuk, ready one, two....three musik!"

Charles walked down the aisle and got Joyce. He gracefully escorted her to the front stairs. Then, it was dad's cue. *Jesu Joy of Mans Desiring* was playing on the two harps and the grand piano. Father, majestically and cautiously, escorted me to the front of the church. He was silently praying the whole time. I could tell because his bottom chin was quivering and he mumbled. He does that when he has gone beyond his comfort zone. He finally brought me to the front. We waited a couple of seconds for the music to stop playing. Dad gave my hand to Reggie. Dad nodded, smiled at Charles, my maiden of honor who was standing next to me, then, took his seat. Oh, I was so proud of all of them, dad, Reggie, and Charles.

The pastor opened his mouth and said, "In the name of the Father, the Son, and the Holy Ghost. We are gathered here today to witness a miracle, the miracle of love, the defining thread that binds a man and his wife together, with his family, under one house and under God."

He continued, "We come together in the name of love unto salvation. As Christ died for the sins of mankind in his everlasting love, so must a man die in the shedding of his love to his wife. As he was resurrected by faith in God, so must a husband and wife resurrect their new life together. Reggie and Sonthy, pray with me. Let us all bow our heads and pray. Everybody, repeat after me, 'Dear heavenly Father, we come to you in the name of Jesus Christ. We acknowledge that Jesus is your Son, and that his blood was shed for our sins. We ask him into our hearts to give us perfect love,' and all say Amen."

Everybody in the church prayed out loud with us. At that moment I knew that everybody really loved me. To pray with me, I could feel their love like a huge energy wave pouring fourth towards Reggie and me.

The pastor continued, "If any man have just cause to believe that this man and this woman should not be bond together in holy matrimony, speak now or forever hold your peace."

Not one person spoke a word. One could have heard a pin drop. It was so quiet, except for the rustling of the television cameramen that were broadcasting the wedding on every channel in the country.

The pastor continued, "The ring please."

Joyce brought out the ring and gave it to the pastor who gave it to Reggie. Reggie slipped the ring on my wedding finger. I started to sniff a little, I felt tears swelling up in me. I couldn't help it.

The pastor expressly said, "Do you, Prince Reggie Wheat, take this woman, Princess Sonthy Savitry, as your lawful, wedded wife? Do you promise to love her, honor her, respect her, and cherish her above all others, keeping your relationship sacred before God and man, through sickness and through health, for richer or for poorer, until death do you part?"

I heard Reggie with great confidence say, "I do!"

"Do you, Princess Sonthy Savitry, take Prince Reggie Wheat, as your lawful, wedded husband? Do you promise to love him, honour him, respect him, and cherish him above all others, keeping your relationship sacred before God and man, through sickness and through health, for richer or for poorer, until death do you part?"

I quickly said, "I do."

"By the power invested in me by God, the state, and the church…..I now pronounce you man and wife. You may now kiss the bride."

Reggie slowly pulled my veil off my head, and with a gentle hand, he kissed me. I yanked him into me and gave him my deep wine down into his everlasting fountain of youth. My speech element explored his moist mouth. My fire was ignited, it blew up in me and left me dizzy, weak in the knees and perpetually turned on. We kissed for about five minutes. The pastor cleared his throat, we finally stopped kissing and looked up.

The pastor said, "Will you two turn around."

We turned around and faced the audience.

He politely continued and said, "I now present to you, Mr. and Mrs Sonthy and Reggie Savitry."

The royal singers sung praises through Handle's *Alleluia Chorus*. The music fragrantly filled the church as we walked down the aisle. Everybody stood up and shouted. As I walked by the televisions and glanced at them, I watched the nation shout and sing. It was just marvelous!

We positioned ourselves at the end of the aisle and greeted our guests as they went by. It took us about an hour and a half to take pictures. After the pictures, the Royal Carriage took Reggie, dad, Joyce, and I through the streets until we got back to the palace.

Many of the people already arrived at the palace for the reception before we did. The reception was held in the main hall at the royal palace, next to the swimming pool. The main hall was around the back of the palace. It could hold 2500 people. The hall had soft, grey and purple walls. The designs on the walls were gold-colored roses. There were twenty large chandeliers hanging from glass domes. Large fifteen-foot windows, along the south, east, and west walls, gushed sunshine in the hall. The sun glittered off the chandeliers and sprayed bright, sparkling colors throughout the hall. The floors were checkered white and gold marble. The drapes were purple with pink and peach rose designs weaved into the fabric.

The tables were round, glass tables that could seat eight people. They were decorated with purple linen table cloths and crystal candle operas. The candles were ivory color. Each table had cards, telling where the guests were to be seated. There were fifteen hosts who escorted people to their tables. I saw that the kitchen crew used our new china, stemware, and diningware on the tables. I was happy about that.

The china we had picked was Royal Albert Diningware. The style was Moonlight Rose. Reed and Barton made the Diningware and the style was called Halo. The stemware was made by Oneida and the style was called Chateau Gold. As the guests arrived and were seated, dad's servants walked around with glasses of champagne and served the guests. We finally arrived, and the entire hall gave us a standing ovation. When it quieted down, I said, "Where is the food? I'm hungry!"

Of course, we couldn't eat right away because dad had to make his speeches. Thank God that only lasted fifteen minutes!

The food was a self-serve buffet dinner, prepared by the royal kitchen. The servants, who brought trays of food around like mobile buffets, served our guests. The people served themselves as the carts came around.

When one of the servants came to our table and opened the tray, the smoked haddock with rice and mushrooms made my mouth water. The beef stroganoff called to me. It knew I was really hungry. The colorful variety of vegetables and fruits kept me quiet while I ate them.

During the dinner, Joyce offered up a toast to us.

She said, "I'm going to make a toast. I know the ten hours of labor pains to get that thirteen-pound baby boy out was enough joy to last a lifetime. I propose that Reggie and Sonthy will give me as much joy as Reggie has since I first held him in my arms. Let all Heaven bless this union!"

Everybody held up their glasses and made "ooh" and "aah" sounds. It was a good time for her speech. I was feeling a little sappy, myself. During the dinner, a string quartet played much soft, classical music in the background. I blamed the dinner music for the sappy mood.

I glanced over at Reggie. He seemed to look like he wasn't feeling well. Maybe it was something in the dinner. He looked fine and handsome, but I sensed that his mood had changed. I put my hand on his leg and whispered, "Are you okay, Honey?"

He said, "I'm feeling a little warm. I feel my energy depleting. I think I need some sugar. Let's cut the cake."

We cut the cake and fed each other a piece.

Dad had every restaurant serve people free food and celebrate with us. The streets were still packed with people.

The dance began at eight o'clock that evening. Reggie and I had some time to ourselves. We talked about our future, especially things we wanted to do after the war. We wanted to have two children: a boy and a girl. I was going to call the boy Reggie, Jr., and Reggie wanted to call the girl Grace.

Reggie looked like he wanted to say something important. He looked at me in that way, really serious and tender.

I said, "What is it, Hon?"

He quietly replied, "I want you to know, that the Brotherhood Company has placed all new organs in me, except for my brain. For the past twenty-five years, I've been their leading experimental pig. I have been completely genetically engineered. That's why I only need less than two hours of sleep every night. That is also why I'm so strong. My top running speed is fifty-five miles per hour. I can leap seventy-five feet straight up. If I get shot, the wound heals immediately. I'm supposed to live 950 years. After that, I'm supposed to get some more new organs and keep living another 950 years. I'm their first living prototype of immortality. I suspect that the sleeping clones are immortals, also. If they sleep with a mortal, it will kill the mortal. Their immortal genetic codes will infect the mortals, like a virus, and the mortals will die within two years. They won't be sick. They will just die. It's a genetic weapon for biological warfare. Any mortal which the clones have sex with will die. Devin and Dylan called it 'the birth of the genetic apocalypse.' They have a hidden army of superior immortals hidden inside some mountain. The plan is to create a superior immortal white race that will rule the earth. Devin and Dylan told us that the 'world thought that we were creating organs in the name of medicine, but we were really creating superior immortals that would help us rule the world.'

The Brotherhood plans to have all their soldiers have sex with the mortals so that they will kill them and take over the world! Sonthy, we have to find them and destroy them! We also have to destroy the sleeping clones."

"But Reggie, you just can't kill people. We will wake the clones. We will kill only those who kill other people. You just can't kill people because you think they are dangerous. We have to find out if they are or not."

"It was the completion of the human genetic map that started this whole apocalypse stuff. Sonthy, if you sleep with me, you will die in two years. Your genetic code will be screwed up! You will have the genetic virus. Oh, my head hurts. I have to lie down."

Reggie went to a back room and lied down for about an hour and a half. I went to talk to dad about the new information Reggie had given me.

Everybody left and went to get ready for the dance. Dad gave the entire country time off from work for two days so they could party with us.

When Reggie woke up, he was feeling like himself, again. We changed clothes. We all had a meeting. We talked about what Reggie said. Dad informed his people, the FBI, CIA, and the Pentagon. Dad had President George Bush, Jr. came over and talked with us, along with Queen Elizabeth, The Israeli Prime minister, and some of the top military officials who came to the wedding.

It was seven forty-five in the evening. All the guests were returning. The servants directed them to the ballroom. The family and I went to the ballroom and stood by the doors to greet everybody. There was an open bar at the end of the ballroom. Many people conglomerated at the bar, others sat down at the tables next to the big band.

The big band played all kinds of music, from classics to modern rock. Reggie and I started the dance by dancing the first dance together. Dad and Joyce came strutting their stuff alongside of us. Joyce and I switched partners. I got to dance with dad, and Reggie danced with his mother. Everybody started joining in. Before long, the floor was full.

It was about one o'clock in the morning. People were still lively and a little inebriated. Reggie and I went around and talked to as many people as we could. We had promised to dance with each other at one o'clock. So, we tied up our conversations and met each other on the dance floor at about ten minutes after one. They were playing our song, *My Golden Promise.*

I loved that song. Whenever I heard it, I felt all gooey inside for Reggie, I would sing that song to him.

"Reggie, did you ask them to play 'My Golden Promise?'"

He just grined that beautiful smile and continued dancing. I started singing along with the lyrics…..

How can I begin - to love you - in the morning
When you leave - my heart - in the air?

Should I spread my love- in the midst - of the night
And give - my soul - to your heart.

I'm gonna hold you
gonna love you
Till I die (My Golden Promise)

Who will care for my tears - when they run - like the rivers -
When they pour - on the shores- like the rain -

Can your love - build the bridge - that we both - will cross on
Can we build - our visions and our dreams

I'm gonna hold you
gonna love you
Till I die (My Golden Promise)"

I cast my love like the wind - never knowing - where it's going
Will you leave me - in the winter- when it's cold

Fools will always love - like a flame - in the evening
Like the milk - in my mind - colored gold

I'm gonna hold you
gonna love you
Till I die (My Golden Promise)

I was in the middle of repeating the last chorus the second time, when Reggie dropped to the floor!

I screamed, "Help! Somebody help me! Dad! Call the house doctor! I checked his pulse. It was weak and irregular. He was barely breathing. I was scared to death. I kept mumbling, "No, no! You've got to stay alive! Not yet! Not yet! God you can't do this to me!"

The doctor came. Thank God he was at the party. Ten minutes later, the ambulance came. People were crowded in a big circle around us. I heard everybody sigh and chatter, Oh, no! Joyce was on the floor, on top of him, crying.

I yelled out, "Dad, can you get her, please! Everybody give us some space! Let the ambulance guys through!"

The EMT guys came, put an IV in him, placed him on a gurney and quickly rolled him through the crowd of vicariously curious onlookers. They loaded him into the ambulance. WKCC, WGCC, and KTCI news were all over us. My heart was pounding. I pushed the cameramen aside and climbed into the ambulance with Reggie. I sat by his head as I watched the guys do their stuff. The doctor, dad, and Joyce quickly got into the ambulance. The police escorted the ambulance to the hospital.

People were out on the streets holding stick-made crosses, with white handkerchiefs tied to them. The people waved the crosses back and forth as the ambulance drove by. Women and children were hugging each other, crying.

The ambulance screeched into the hospital's emergency lot! The guys quickly hauled Reggie out. Dr. Shakina, the royal doctor, continued to work on Reggie the whole time. They took tissue and blood samples from him and tried to stabilize him. After about an hour, things looked good. They transferred him to the inpatient floor.

Security suddenly became tight on that floor. Reporters tried to interview us, but Dad told the royal guards not to let it happen. They blocked of the whole floor and didn't let anyone come or go, except medical personnel.

Everybody was very sweet to us. Queen Elizabeth II, George Bush, Jr., and the Prime Minister of Israel were all present. Dad let them through. Dad spoke with them for a little bit, and they stayed out in the hall for hours. They brought accommodations for everybody and we waited. Reggie was sleeping. We all sat there the whole night, waiting for Reggie to wake up.

At six thirty in the morning, he woke up with a smile. His long eyelashes opened like butterfly wings as his blue eyes scanned the room. His voice was strong.

He said, "Sonthy, I'm dying. I saw your mother and spoke with her. She is standing next to you. I know you can't see her, but she says that she is here to escort me home to our Heavenly Father."

I started to cry.

I said, "Mom, ask God to give us a week, huh! We just got married! I still want to have a honeymoon!" I was trembling and scared.

Reggie calmly looked at me and smiled, then gently said, "It's okay. Bring Charles in here."

I went out in the hall and called Charles.

"Charles, Reggie wants to talk to you."

Charles came in, very sorrowfully, with his head down. Reggie looked at him and said, "Charles will you forgive me for treating you so mean? I know you are a good guy, and you love my Sonthy. God told me when I was out walking the light. Give me your hand."

Charles gave Reggie his right hand. Reggie took it and grabbed my right hand and said, "Charles, take care of my Sonthy and my twins in her belly. I want you to call them Reggie Jr, and Grace."

Charles started to cry. I started to cry. Reggie was his usually strong self. Joyce was hugging dad and sniffling.

Charles said, "Reggie, I forgave you a long time ago. I want you to know that. I will take care of your Sonthy."

Reggie patted Charles on the chest, twice, and said, "Now, you get out of the room. I have to talk to my wife."

"Honey, come over close to the bed and shut the door."

I told dad and Joyce to wait outside. I closed the door behind me. The minute I closed the door, mom showed up.

"Mom! I can see you! It's not seventy years yet!"

"Yes, Dear. I know. I've been watching you. Jesus is going to grant your request. I'll be back next Friday to take your husband home with me. Do as Reggie says. I love you very much. You have a long road ahead of you. Kill those people you need to kill.

Prevent this genetic apocalypse. That group of immortals Reggie told you about? They are in the middle of Mount Everest. Get them, and destroy them. You have to create something to keep mankind alive. Now, quit wasting time and do it! You have a war going on down here! Give me a hug."

I gave my mama a hug and I cried some more. I told her I would be strong and I would do it. She kissed me, and I watched her walk into the light, through the hospital window.

Reggie took my hand, and said, "Do you still want a honeymoon?"

I said, "Yes."

"Then we will have the honeymoon in our suite here at the hospital. I'm not strong enough to be about. But my heart is strong enough to make love to you."

That whole week we made love. I had learned many secrets about my husband that the years had hidden. Never again would I know that love could be so addicting. It was madness! But it was the greatest high I had ever felt. My anger and sorrow stayed with me for many months.

It was eleven o'clock Friday night when mom showed up. I started crying again, but mom said, "Hush child! Don't you see the Morning Star standing there?" I looked up, and the angel was holding out his arms to receive Reggie. I saw Reggie sigh his last breath as his spirit left him and went to the angel who was holding out his arms. Reggie and I made eye contact for two minutes as he silently stood between mom and the angel. He didn't say a word, but I heard everything he had to say. The angel, mom, and Reggie all walked into the light. I got on my knees, bent over, sobbing and wailing. I was happy and sad at the same time. I wanted to be the one that was taken. I felt so alone, like a deep void. A black hole just shattered my world. As I looked up, I saw the third Heavens open, and they walked under that giant pearl. The pearl slowly came down between the huge golden wall. I knew it was over. My darkness collapsed on me suddenly. I couldn't breath. I was lying in a ball curled up on the floor whimpering, "Jesus! My life is over. Help me, Jesus! Oh God, help me!"

I heard this deep strong voice fill the room,

In isolation and great fear I said, "Who is that? Is that you Lord?"

He said, "I am, that I am. I am Alpha and Omega, the Cornerstone that the builders rejected. Stand upon thy feet and be thou strong, for I shall surely go before thee. Now, go in thy faith and be of good cheer for I am with thee."

Even though my knees were weak, I felt some warm glow bring me to my feet, as if my body had it's own mind. The door opened on it's own, and dad came running to meet me. I collapsed in his arms and sobbed, pitifully.

That Sunday, we buried Reggie on the Island of Patmos. It was the darkest, dreariest, and wettest day of my life! The funeral was awful. I don't even want to talk about it, before I started crying, again.

Reggie, Jr. and Grace were born exactly nine months later, to the day after their father's death, in the same hospital room. I requested that room. Now, that day has two special meanings to me. The seed that was sown in death was now alive in two more children! Ha!

As I sat up in that hospital bed holding my two newborns, I thought out loud, "Shit! It's time to kick some fucking ass! I will walk into the light with pride!"

ABOUT THE AUTHOR

"Bob was born in Liberia, West Africa, and lived there for eight years before he came to America in 1970. He says that for his first eight years, he lived "in the jungle" and I have heard him describe his life in his rural village very vividly. His experiences in that environment are a source of comparison and contrast for him, enabling him to look at American culture from an unusual perspective." After Bob came to America, he began negotiating the American public school system. He spoke no English when he was placed in the second grade. He managed to overcome this considerable problem, however, with a few years of private tutoring, he eventually skipped the eighth grade and went on his way to graduating from high school. After high school, he worked for a few years and then joined the Navy for four years, from 1988-1992. His tour of duty in the Navy provided him with GI Bill benefits, enabling him to go to college."

"Deswin has a special rapport with different age groups. Deswin always gets the students emotionally and physically involved in his performances,"

...**Dr. Niedzwiecki**, Assistant Professor, UW - La Crosse.

"He [Mr. Gbala] has such an abundance of creative energy that, if he were somehow blocked in his creative endeavors, he might well explode!"

...**Dr. Laura Nelson**, Chair, Professor, UW - La Crosse.

"In spite of his animation and energy he pours into his storytelling, none can be as fascinating as the true story of Gbala's first eight years of life,"

...**Pat Moore**, La Crosse Tribune.